P9-AGN-445

TWICE UPON A PREQUEL
& Three Shorts

DERALD W. HAMILTON

D HAMILTON B(

Twice Upon a Prequel & Three Shorts

© 2011 Derald W. Hamilton
All Rights Reserved

*Editors:Kimberly   Rufer-bach,   Michelle   Pollace,
Sonia Shell, Mary Linn Roby, Becky Hayes, Jo Sarti,
Lynne Thomas Adler, and Olga Perez*

Cover and book design by Rebecca Hayes
www.rebeccahayes.us

Published in the United States by
D Hamilton Books
Campbell, CA
www.dhamiltonbooks.com

ISBN 978-0-9846192-1-4

Library of Congress Control Number 2011961067

Dedicated to Nobody in Particular…

ACKNOWLEDGEMENTS

Presentation of this second literary endeavor would not be complete without my having acknowledged all the great and wonderful people who availed me of their talent, patience, insight, and invaluable feedback. It is to these folks that I again render my heartfelt thanks and gratitude.

To Todd Rothbard who provided me with low rent shelter while I was in the throes of creativity. To Kimberly Rufer-bach, Michelle Pollace, Sonia Shell, Mary Linn Roby, Becky Hayes, Jo Sarti, Lynne Thomas Adler, and Olga Perez for their editing assistance.

Special thanks to: Jo Sarti for my first publishing opportunity, Sonia Shell for providing me with a musical outlet, and to Amy Surdacki for providing me with spiritual parameters.

To Alexander Clerk and Barbara Grover for helping me keep my psychological balance.

To Becky Hayes for her magnificent cover design and assistance in the publishing of this novel.

To Lynne Thomas Adler and Kory Trebbin. I'd have been lost if you guys weren't there to help me with this @#$%% computer and all it's #&*%^ups.

And lastly, but far from least, I'd like to express my supreme gratitude to all you readers out there, and it is my sincere wish and desire to make this read worth your while.

CONTENTS

THE ASTONISHING
ELMO PIGGINS

1

Elmo Piggins' story is what could most likely be construed as a portrait of single-mindedness. Regardless of the era a single-minded individual frequents, his or her tale remains a timely one. For instance, take the Apostle Paul: after being struck blind on the road to Damascus, while beholding a vision and revelation of Christ, his single-minded purpose throughout the rest of his life was the spreading of the Gospel and tending to the things of God. As an end result to Paul's single-minded devotion to this cause, his name has been revered through the ages, and his letters have been canonized prominently among the scriptures.

Visions of Christ do tend to radically alter a person's life. Twentieth-century author Jack Kerouac had a similar vision of Christ in an altered state of consciousness at Big Sur, California, that resulted in his giving up of myriad vices, renouncing his bohemian lifestyle, and returning to his Catholic roots.

On the dark side of the single-minded spectrum, we have Captain Ahab, a man whose sole obsession was the seeking out and killing of the great white whale, Moby Dick. Such an obsession inevitably led to his destruction and the deaths of all on board his ship, save one. But on a positive note, Captain Ahab has also been extolled in the annals of American literature as perhaps the most powerful literary figure ever created.

Like Paul and Ahab, Elmo Piggins was not *born* with this sense of single-mindedness. It was something he acquired as he reached a certain point in his maturation. Elmo grew up in and around Georgetown County, South Carolina, in the middle of the twentieth century. He was the son of the Reverend Elwood Piggins, a minister who served as associate pastor, executive pastor, and minister in a number of the mainstream churches in the Georgetown area.

Elmo was a typical child—thin-framed, sandy-haired, freckle-faced, gangly, and plain looking, with mischievous ways hardly befitting a preacher's kid. He liked to play about the marshes and the beach area near his home, where he would bodysurf on the waves, climb the palmetto, dogwood, and magnolia trees, and comb the beach for shells and other artifacts that drew his interest. By the time he was six, he had broken his left arm, gotten stung by a jellyfish, pinched by a crab, and bitten by a snake, and all the other forms of wildlife he brought home hoping his parents would allow him to keep as pets.

Yet, even though Elmo's exploits were colorful ones for a boy his age, they were massively eclipsed by those of his older sister, Lawanda, who was seven years his senior. Lawanda was a free spirit whose inclinations ran counter to the communal mores that surrounded her. She would paint mural scenes on public buildings of naked youths frolicking about in pastoral settings with garlands of flowers in their hair. The paintings were masterfully done, yet many of the town's folks deemed them inappropriate by community standards. She was a chronic violator of curfew. But most noticeably, she selected a circle of friends who were amongst the town's undesirables. She definitely did not fit the image of a minister's daughter.

Even her appearance went contrary to the norms. Before she entered her teens, she dressed in the styles that were prevalent among her singing idols, like Joni Mitchell, Jennifer Warnke, Lynn Kellogg, Judi Collins, Bob Dylan, and Joan Baez. Her auburn hair was long, flowing, and often adorned with beads, flowers, or bandanas.

Even before the age of puberty, her looks reflected a curious mixture of troubled innocence and smoldering sensuality. Her parents tried to ride herd on these outward appearances and attitudes, and would rebuke her sternly for giving off the wrong signals, but Lawanda was exceedingly strong-willed and always one step ahead of their efforts. Often times she could be seen leaving the house dressed in the conventional attire of blue jeans and a modest blouse, carrying a guitar case and/or backpack where she stashed her more colorful clothes. Then, after she had eluded her parents' watchful eyes, she would change into her preferred mode of dress.

The hippie mannerisms, guitar playing, and musical compositions she chose to play were always running afoul of school protocol. There were times when her behavioral attributes could be successfully channeled into the school's student artistic programs, but even her artistic accomplishments were known to overstep the boundaries of acceptability and the parameters of good taste. In one instance, she drew a portrait spoofing *The Last Supper,* and of course, there were always her pictures that portrayed "free love." Instances such as these frequently resulted in her being sent to the principal's office for disciplinary measures. Corporal punishment was still in vogue at her school, and Lawanda was no stranger to its enforcement; this was a frequent experience throughout her grade-school years and beyond.

Once she was in the principal's office, she would be greeted by the stern countenance of a balding, forty-plus man in a gray suit with a middle-age paunch. He would grimace as Lawanda had seen countless times before. "Lawanda Piggins, again?" he would say. "Same thing, lewd artwork. You'd think you'd have learned by now. And a preacher's daughter. Well, you know the drill. Bend over." And the principal would retrieve his paddle from his desk to deliver firm blows to her posterior region. As he delivered the blows, he disclosed, "Sometimes, I wonder if I'm making any kind of impression at all on you by doing this." He would continue, punctuating his soliloquy with firm swats to Lawanda's behind. "We work so hard trying to extol the values and virtues of decent *swat!* Christian living amongst you students *swat!* and try our damndest to *swat!* matriculate good, *swat!* God-fearing citizens of the future, *swat!* and then a foul ball like you comes along. *swat!* I swear, it makes me feel like *swat!* such a failure. I feel like all my efforts *swat!* are so futile at times. And that just *swat!* depresses me no end."

Lawanda would say nothing in response to his words. All she could feel was pain.

2

Church and Sunday school were entities Lawanda hated with her whole heart. The perceived triteness of her father's sermons grated unmercifully upon her independent spirit to the point where she often felt like screaming.

Lawanda's Sunday school teacher also touched her in ways she did not feel comfortable. She tried to report these incidents, but was rebuffed and rebuked by both her parents and others in the church for her efforts. Her mother, Mrs. Ellen Piggins, a medium-built woman a couple years younger than her husband, might have been the first to lend credence to Lawanda's claim were it not for the fact that this particular Sunday school teacher had a reputation that was beyond reproach. This attribute, in and of itself, gave her more cause to lend credibility to the teacher's denial than to Lawanda's accusations.

Her father, a sturdily built man in his mid-thirties, was endowed with a slight paunch and a graying and persistently receding hairline. Being the minister, he consistently demanded that both she and Elmo attend all services and was particularly zealous when it came to seeing that they were both baptized by the age of seven, the age of accountability. As a matter of the denomination doctrine Reverend Elwood Piggins rigidly ascribed to – the Cambellite tradition, with a little St. Augustine thrown in for good measure – the ritual of baptism was essential for the remittance of sin, and no salvation could be attained without submission to it. Elmo quietly complied with his father's wishes when it came his time to be baptized. Lawanda, on the other hand, fought her father in this ritual like one possessed of the devil. She struggled against being brought into the baptistery: she screamed, "Let me go!" and let out a few expletives in the process. This occurred on several occasions, much to the embarrassment and chagrin of both her parents and the church elders. Eventually, God had to call Elwood to another church because of her conduct.

Once situated in the new church, Elwood and his wife Ellen sat Lawanda down in the living room one Saturday evening. Elwood was the first to speak. "Lawanda, we've arranged for you to be baptized tomorrow. Now, this is a new church, so your mother and I want you to behave yourself this time and allow yourself to be baptized without incident."

Lawanda's voice was fraught with vehement protest, "I don't want to be baptized!" she shouted.

Elwood's voice was stern, "Lawanda, you're

almost eight years old, and you know as well as I do that the time to be baptized is seven. And it doesn't look very good for a minister's daughter to defy the will of her parents in this matter."

"I don't care!" she shouted once again.

Her mother, Ellen Piggins, then broke into the conversation. She had auburn hair that she usually wore tucked back in a bun. It had been a few months since she had given birth to Elmo, so she was not yet back in shape. "Dear," she said. Her voice was soft and conciliatory, "your father and I are only doing this for your own good, because we love you and we don't want our daughter burning in Hell."

Lawanda remained adamant as she folded her arms tightly. "I don't even believe in that stuff!"

He mother continued to speak in her warm and appeasing manner. "You may not believe in it, but that doesn't make it any less true."

Elwood then broke in with a brusque tone, "Look, young lady, you are going to be baptized tomorrow, and that's it. Now, I don't want any more arguments out of you, and I definitely don't want any acting out when it comes your time to be baptized! I will ask if you've accepted the Lord Jesus Christ as your personal savior. You will say yes."

"But he's not my personal savior!" Lawanda protested.

Elwood remained adamant, "He *is* your Lord and personal savior, and I will not have you say otherwise!"

"And if I do?" Lawanda said, testing the waters.

"Then so help me, young lady, when I get you home, you're going to feel my belt against your rear end so hard you won't be able to sit down for a month, and I believe you know me well enough to know that I mean it."

Elmo, though less than a year old, took in this volatile encounter between his parents and his sister from his playpen, and was able to draw the following conclusions: 1) The wrath of God equals the wrath of parents; 2) Jesus, whoever he is, is not one to be denied, unless you want a sore butt courtesy of an irate parent.

As for Lawanda, she did indeed know her father usually made good on such threats, and between home and school she was indeed no stranger to pain in the posterior. So, that Sunday, when it came her time to be baptized, she was ever so willing to concede to her parents' wishes, gave open testimony before the congregation to Jesus being her personal Lord and savior, and was then immersed in the waters.

3

Lawanda commanded more artistic talents than painting. The talent that truly stood out was her penchant for music. As early as grade school, she was labeled a musical prodigy. Her singing was without peer in the school's glee club and chorus, and as for musical instruments, even without the benefit of lessons, she was able to naturally pick up any stringed instrument, piano, organ, harpsichord, and a variety of percussion instruments. At the age of nine, her parents bought her an acoustic guitar that she would play for hours at a time. She composed her own music and performed publicly for her friends in open-air concerts at the park and drew many onlookers as a result. Her father often tried to coax her into playing for the church. One time he approached her on the matter while she was sitting on the back porch practicing her guitar. She looked up at him and said, "Dad, I don't think the church would like to hear the songs I sing."

"Then sing some Christian songs," Elwood replied. "You know, songs like 'Amazing Grace' or 'What a Friend We Have In Jesus.'"

"You've got to be kidding," Lawanda winced at

her dad's suggestion.

Elwood rebuked his daughter, "Lawanda, there is nothing wrong with you performing songs like that! Matter of fact, it just might do you some good!"

Lawanda let out a sharp, "Ha! Just like baptism did me good? All it got me was wet and embarrassed!"

Angered by his daughter's attitude, Elwood pointed his finger at her in stern reproach and said, "One day, there's going to come a reckoning for that kind of attitude!" Elwood then turned abruptly and walked away. He was never successful at getting her to perform in church and finally gave up on any hope of success in his efforts. After all, it took all the pressure he was able to conjure up just to get her to attend services on Sunday.

4

By the age of thirteen, Lawanda and some of her neighborhood friends formed a rock band. At times, the band indulged in semi-quiet folk-rock favorites the older members of the community could begrudgingly tolerate. But there were many more times when musical amplification that accompanied their hard-rock tunes would raise the community's ire. Elwood was often inundated with complaints about the noise level coming from his garage.

Other problems were soon to accompany Lawanda's penchant for loud music. One day, Ellen was cleaning up Lawanda's room when she found, amid Lawanda's clothes, a "roach" clip, a hash pipe, an eighth of an ounce of marijuana, and some cocaine wrapped in a plastic bag. That evening she brought the matter to Elwood's attention. Elwood was quick to react.

He cornered Lawanda in the den, where she was playing her guitar.

"Lawanda," he snapped.

Lawanda looked up and faced her father.

"Your mother was going through your clothes today and found a few things that concern us."

"So?" was Lawanda's rejoinder. Her facial expression exuded a look of contempt and defiance.

"I believe we talked to you and your brother about the dangers of drugs."

"Yeah, you did. I thought it was a bunch of shit."

"Young lady," Elwood countered, "I can't control the language you use with your friends, but I will *not* tolerate you speaking to me or your mother in that manner! Now, I want to know where you got the drugs. Who gave them to you, and where can I find him?"

"Fuck you!" Lawanda barked back.

Elwood took the belt from around his waist and joined the two ends of the belt with his hand. He then looked squarely at Lawanda and spoke with deliberation in his voice, "I told you I would not tolerate that kind of talk. I'm going to ask you once again, where did you get that dope? You can tell me now and save yourself some pain, or so help me, I'll beat it out of you! I'd prefer the former to the latter, because I hold no joy in having to whip my children!"

"Oh, come on, now," Lawanda retorted, "you're not going to spank me. I'm thirteen now. Fathers don't whip thirteen-year-old daughters."

Elwood moved toward Lawanda with belt in hand. "I don't care if you're eighty-five years old and ready for your second wheelchair! If I feel you need a whipping, I'll give you one! So you can spare yourself a lot of pain by telling me who it was who gave you that dope!"

Lawanda grinned defiantly, "You're bluffing."

"No, I'm not," Elwood replied. He then grabbed Lawanda by the arm and pulled her over his knee. He raised his arm high, then swiftly brought the belt down against her rear end rendering a sharp, piercing *THWACK!* Again and again he beat her rear end with his belt. Lawanda began to shriek, then she started to curse, until finally, the pain became so intense and excruciating that she begged him to stop.

"Stop! Daddy, please! I'll tell! I'll tell!" she shrieked.

Elwood let her up.

Tears were still rolling down her face. Her breathing was swift and erratic. Her voice trembled, and she stammered, "I-it was Lenny Pizer! He gave it to me!" And she told him where he lived. It was on the other side of town in a more unsavory area.

'"Okay, young lady," Elwood replied. "You're grounded until further notice. Now go to your room."

Lawanda hurried tearfully out of the den toward her room.

Elwood retired to the living room where he reached into the wall safe and pulled out his handgun, a weapon he had not used in ages. Elmo, barely six years old, was descending the staircase and caught a glimpse of his father handling the gun. He saw Elwood disassembling the gun. His father began to clean the gun and Elmo could tell by the practiced, sure movement of his father's hands that he knew what he was doing—it was, in fact, a reflection of his father's military training.

Elmo then witnessed his father load a clip with ammunition and don his jacket, tucking the gun into the inner pocket. The sight of his father in the throes of such a calm yet violent act left an indelible impression upon Elmo's susceptible, young psyche. "God have mercy," he heard his father say under his breath. "It's every father's worst nightmare to have to do this, but tonight I've got to."

Elwood left the living room, heading toward the front door. Ellen saw him just before he was about to leave.

"Elwood," she said, "where are you going?"

"Just out for a little drive."

"Elwood, don't lie to me! You're going after her supplier. Please don't! I don't want you getting hurt! I don't want you getting in trouble! I don't want… oh God, Elwood! Please!" Tears began rolling down her face as she continued to plead.

"Dear," he said, taking her in his arms. "evil does not go away on its own. It has to be confronted."

Ellen backed off, feeling the lump in his inner pocket. She knew what that meant and the thought sickened her with grief. "You're taking that gun! Elwood, you promised me!"

Again Elwood extended his arms in an attempt to comfort his sobbing wife. "Dear, it'll be all right. I'll exercise every precaution. But this is something that has to be done."

"But what about the police?" She asked. "Shouldn't you notify the police first?"

"Ellen," Elwood replied in a sharp tone, "the police won't do squat! They have to catch him in the act! But there's nothing that says I have to be that lenient."

"Elwood," she cried, "don't go!"

"Don't try to stop me!" Elwood sharply countered. "I'm doing my job! Defending our home!"

Elmo watched in the shadows as Elwood turned and walked out the door.

5

Elwood drove his car to a run-down bar located on the east end of town. From the parking lot he could hear the blare of rock music and the boisterous resonance of rowdy voices. As he drew nearer, the knot in his stomach tightened. He feared this place, particularly at night. This was not, he knew, a safe place to be. In fact, a few killings had taken place here last year. Taking a deep breath he went inside. The place reeked with the smell of marijuana, spilled booze and urine. Its occupants were definitely not the sort seen at church socials. Finding Lenny Pizer amid this unsavory crowd would not, he realized, be an easy task, even if he were here.

"Could you tell me where I could find a Lenny Pizer?" he asked a coarse husk of a man.

"Who wants to know?" he said glaring at Elwood.

"The father of one of his customers."

The man laughed, "And you think I'm just gonna point him out to you?"

Elwood reached inside his jacket, pulled out his gun and stuck it against the man's rib cage. "I'd sure appreciate it if you would," he said.

The man's face dropped its mask of bravado as he pointed over to the far wall. "H-happy to. He's the one sitting with those two broads over there."

"Thank you. Your cooperation is most appreciated." Elwood put his gun back into his jacket pocket, and headed toward Lenny Pizer. A scant second later, the man behind Elwood grabbed a chair, lifted it over his head and prepared to launch it in Elwood's direction. Elwood turned abruptly, grasping his firearm from inside his pocket. "I would not advise following through with what I think you're about to do. Evil actions harbor bitter consequences." The man, after a brief pause, gently set the chair back down on the floor, smiled, and turned away. Elwood then turned in the direction of Lenny Pizer. Once again he took in a deep breath and released it. A few more steps found him standing at Lenny's table.

"Lenny Pizer?" He inquired, standing with one hand loosely holding the gun in his pocket.

Lenny Pizer was a grungy, unshaven man between the ages of nineteen and twenty-three, by Elwood's observation. His long, dingy, light brown hair fell down the back of his shoulders. His dirty jeans, wrinkled T-shirt, and scuffed shoes seemed to accentuate the malign nature of his personality. "Yeah?" Lenny replied in a somber, threatening tone, eyeing Elwood's hidden hand.

Elwood then motioned to the women sitting with Lenny. "Lenny and I have something to discuss in private. Would you two please leave?"

"Sure," one of the women replied, and the two of them left the table.

Lenny glared at Elwood. "This had better be pretty damn important, old man!"

"It is," Elwood responded. "I'm Lawanda Piggins' father."

Lenny rose immediately from his chair, slamming his fist on the table. "I knew that goddamn bitch would be trouble!"

Elwood felt a bit edgy and rage was beginning to surface as he absorbed the impact of Lenny's words and demeanor. "I can be rather persuasive when it comes to getting information from my daughter. Oh, and I don't appreciate you using the Lord's name in vain, or referring to my daughter in such a manner. But that's beside the point. I'm here to tell you that if you want to stay healthy, you are not to sell or give my daughter any more drugs."

Lenny grinned and laughed. "Hey, Reverend, I think you're threatening me."

Provoked to anger by Lenny's callous contempt, a sudden sweep of adrenaline washed over Elwood as he forcibly grabbed Lenny by the collar, threw him up against the wall, reached for his gun and pointed it squarely between Lenny's eyes.

"No, I'm not threatening you, you young punk!" Elwood snarled. "I'll kill you if you ever give my daughter any more dope!" Elwood then placed the gun up against the wall by Lenny's ear and fired. There was an abrupt silence in the room.

Lenny broke out in tears. All the color in his face was gone. His body trembled fiercely. Elwood turned and pointed his gun toward the rest of the occupants. "And the same holds true for the rest of you!" After voicing that somber announcement, Elwood tucked the gun back into his inner pocket, turned, and calmly vacated the premises unimpeded by its many inhabitants, who were now silent and watchful.

As far as Elwood could ascertain, that was the last he would see or hear about Lenny Pizer. But, as he was later to discover, Lawanda's free spirit was not something to be so easily suppressed. Elwood could not help but figure that he may have only ignited the flames of alienation to an even greater degree by giving Lawanda a whipping. *A whipping,* he thought, not exactly something you give a thirteen-year-old. Perhaps a more creative form of coercion might have been more effective, but Elwood was at a loss to figure what that might be.

Elwood was right. Lawanda now carried with her heightened feelings of violation and resentment that were more deeply imbedded within her emotionally scarred psyche. Not since her forced baptism had she felt more transgressed, more desecrated… or more inclined toward revenge.

6

A couple of years later, Lawanda and some friends were circled around a campfire at the beach. Lawanda was playing a friend's guitar and entertaining the group with some singing, as she had done so many times in the past. She always held her audience entranced and spellbound by her musical talent, and they were always after her to play their favorites. After the playing ceased, one of the members of the group, a dark-haired boy of about fourteen, reached into his jacket pocket and pulled out a baggy of marijuana, whispering, "I got the Red Bud!"

A slender, red-haired girl of about fifteen held up a small flat package and said, "I've got some Zig Zags!"

Buddy, a skinny guy with glasses, rolled a joint. The crowd all bunched together with great ceremony. Then, in a casual fashion, they began to pass the joint around. Lawanda, on occasion, took prolonged drags and at times needed to be cautioned about Bogart-ing.

"Hey, I entertained you folks for over an hour," Lawanda said. "Let me get a decent buzz."

The crowd laughed as they continued to toke.

As Lawanda attained more and more of a buzz, she began to flirt heavily with Kevin, a certain muscular, blond sixteen-year-old. The momentum of her flirting escalated to a higher and higher degree until impulse claimed them both. They were quick to escape from the group and departed unnoticed.

They began running and skipping in a childlike manner, hand-in-hand down the sidewalk amid the shelter of the pine, oak, and palmetto trees in the dim, fluorescent glow of the streetlights, laughing through their gasps for air. Beads of perspiration began to form on their brows and saturate their clothing.

Their rapid pace continued until the boy began to tire and feel a stitch in his side. "Keep running, you slow poke!" Lawanda cried, taunting him ever onward, laughing, always testing his limitations. She felt a supreme sense of control at this moment and found it to be intoxicating. She enjoyed the power and carried it through to its pinnacle.

Continuing her taunts, much to the chagrin of her male companion, they finally arrived at her house. Her father and mother were attending a church function and she knew they would not be back for two or three hours. She bid her guest to enter, still in a teasing and taunting fashion.

He followed her upstairs where she hastily tore

off her clothes. Her companion hurriedly took her cue. Still breathing heavily, she led him into the bathroom where they showered to wash off the sweat. It was a sultry night, very humid. While showering, they explored one another, lathering each other's bodies and arousing each other's desire, all the while giggling and laughing through their gasps for air, made all the more arduous by the steam that filled the enclosed area. Kevin, at one point, became so aroused that he ejaculated. Lawanda giggled as Kevin blushed.

With both of their inclinations honed to a climactic level, they hastily dried themselves off and moved on to Lawanda's room. They fell onto Lawanda's bed, Kevin on top of her, desperately attempting to synchronize his breathing to hers.

Scant seconds later, her companion found the point of penetration and began pumping into her, smothering her face, neck, ears, and breasts with kisses and licks. Lawanda echoed with unrestrained squeals of ecstasy. Moments after Lawanda experienced her climax, her companion found his release and filled her. They then both lay in each other's arms, laughing and exchanging kisses of varying lengths and intensity. Their breathing began to slow.

Once they had regained a degree of composure, the boy found a renewed sense of arousal. This time

Lawanda wanted to be on top. During this second sizzling lovemaking session, her parents, along with Elmo, arrived home from their church meeting. "I tell you," said Elwood to his wife, "1 never dreamed the pulpit steering committee would find the need to address issues so petty in nature, and talk about them with such fervency. I don't know if all my years in the ministry have prepared me to deal with such stuff. It's like that scene in The Music Man. 'I hear we got a pool table here in River City!'"

"Well, Elwood," Ellen replied, "you'll have to admit, some of those issues have hit home for us. Maybe it is a community issue and can't be left to just the singular family."

"Maybe you're right," Elwood responded, "but..." At that moment, he glanced upward. His gaze hardened as he saw both male and female clothes strewn together on the floor. "What the hell?" He bellowed and rushed up the staircase. As he reached the top of the stairs, he found himself colliding with the teenaged boy, scrambling to retrieve his clothes.

Hearing the commotion, Lawanda rushed from her room with a bed sheet wrapped about her. Elwood focused in on the scene and drew the obvious conclusion.

"You bastard!" He growled as he grabbed the boy and threw him against the wall at the top of the staircase.

"Daddy!" Lawanda cried. "Stop it!"

Elwood then pushed the boy up against the wall and kneed him in the groin.

The boy crumpled over in pain. "Stop what?" Elwood countered. "Stop beating on the son of a bitch who defiled my daughter? Lawanda, I've just begun!" And another blow flew against the boy's face, this one drawing blood. Elwood raised his fist to strike again. It was then that he felt the restraining hand of his wife.

"Dear," Ellen spoke, "he's had enough!"

"Oh, really?" Elwood responded. "So what do you suggest I do now?"

Ellen stepped up to the young man. "What's your name?"

"Kevin Walters," the young man squeaked through his pain.

"Okay," Ellen insisted, "now I want your address and phone number."

"Give it to her!" Elwood commanded.

The young man gave her his address and phone number.

"I believe we should have a talk with your parents. And you," she said pointing to Lawanda, "get dressed. You're coming along."

"No!" Lawanda screamed.

"Yes," Ellen said. "I'll have no arguments from

you, now, young lady! Do as you're told!"

Elmo, as he had done so often in the past, watched and took in everything that was going on about him. As he watched these events unfold before him, he drew the obvious lesson they had to teach him – Don't get caught with your pants down. It seemed like an easy lesson to apply. Of course, young Elmo had not as yet reached puberty, so there was only so much he could know.

As for Lawanda, she turned and walked toward her room. Long ago, she was taught the folly of defiance when her mother delivered a command in a tone so imposing and resolute. The events that were to follow only served to drive an even deeper wedge of estrangement between Lawanda and her parents. The resentment and bitterness swelled to a new level as consequence followed consequence. She was humiliated by the confrontation with Kevin's parents. Shame and rebuke was leveled upon them by both their parents. She was forced to undergo a pregnancy exam and endure the discomfiture her actions brought to her father's ministry.

Knowledge of her misdeeds gradually gained the attention of the congregation. But this would not be the last time that knowledge of Lawanda's sexual activities would come to the attention of her parents. There would be other boys, other encounters, and it would not be long before it would be brought to the awareness of the community that other daughters had followed suit.

Meanwhile, nine-year-old Elmo watched his family address these issues as they surfaced.

7

Georgetown County's concern for the conduct of its teenage progeny began to grow, and youthful rebellion reached its peak a couple of years later. Elwood had mocked its presence that first night to his wife, but fear and concern had now extended itself beyond the stage where he could joke about it. Meanwhile, Lawanda was seventeen and more engrossed than ever in the local pop cultural scene.

Just a few months before Lawanda's senior year, the Reverend Todd Meachum of The Victory Over Evil Christian Fellowship of Georgetown County delivered a dynamic, forthright, hellfire-and-brimstone sermon regarding corruption of the youth of Georgetown and perhaps the nation as a whole. He was a short, capacious man with brown hair, receding hairline, and glasses. He had nowhere near the educational credentials of Elwood Piggins. In fact, rumor was that he never even completed his undergraduate studies. But Reverend Meachum had charisma, a feature that covered a multitude of shortcomings. What Reverend Meachum lacked in physical stature, he made up for in vocal projection and magnetism that poured forth in abundance with dynamic inspiration.

The church building was packed that Sunday to the point where provisions needed to be made to accommodate the overflow of attendees. Chairs and loudspeakers were set up outside. When the supply of chairs for the outside attendees was exhausted, many had to situate themselves on the ground, yet scores of people sat waiting, anxious to hear Reverend Meachum's message. First, the anthem "Victory In Jesus" was rendered. Then a series of hymns were sung, followed by prayers. Finally, the reverend assumed his place at the pulpit. Total silence ensued. "Now, good people," he began, "I would like you to turn in your Bibles to the Book of Deuteronomy, chapter 5, verse 29, and read along with me..."

The congregation fumbled through their Bibles to find the exact passage, while Reverend Meachum expedited the process for himself via the use of numbered bookmarks and highlighted scriptural passages.

Reverend Meachum began reading. "'0 that there were such a heart in them, that they would fear me, and keep all my commandments always, that it might be well with them, and with their children forever.' Now, if you will turn again with me to the Book of Ezekiel, chapter 28, verse 13." Pages turned while someone coughed and a baby cried.

The reverend resumed speaking, "And if I might juxtapose that Satan was created a beautiful, musical creature, 'Every precious stone was thy covering... the workmanship of thy tablets and of thy pipes was prepared in thee in the day that thou wast created.'"

He then looked up from his text, fixed his sights upon the congregation and began addressing them, "So, we see here from scripture that music was built into Lucifer's very nature. Now, my friends, in knowing that, are we foolish enough to make the assumption that given his propensity for evil, he would not use this music to enslave and deceive?"

"Now, my friends," he continued, "let's turn once again in our Bibles to the Apostle Paul's letter to the Ephesians, chapter 5, verses 6 through 8. Read along with me ..."Again the congregation fumbled through their Bibles as Reverend Meachum continued to speak. "'Let not man deceive you with vain word: for because of these things cometh the wrath of God upon the children of disobedience. Be not ye therefore partakers with them. For ye were sometimes darkness, but now are ye light in the Lord: walk as children of light.' And finally, dear brethren, turn again with me to the Epistle to the Hebrews, chapter 3, verse 13 ..." pages rustling, "'but exhort one another daily, while it is called today; lest any of you be hardened through the deceitfulness of sin.' Please bow with me now in prayer." The congregation bowed their heads. "Lord, may the words of my mouth and the meditations of my heart be acceptable in thy sight, 0 Lord. I solemnly beseech thee in the name of Jesus Christ our Lord and Savior, Amen."

Some voices echoed his "Amen." The members of the congregation then lifted their heads and focused on Reverend Meachum, awed by his mastery of the Bible.

Reverend Meachum fixed his eyes on the congregation, "Friends, brethren, and members of the congregation, as I was busy in the preparation of this sermon, my mind went back to my college days and the course I took in biology. Now science was never my strongest suit, but I do remember something that was said by the professor of that class. He said that it has been proven that if a frog were placed into a container of boiling water, that frog would immediately seek to exit that water. But, if that same frog is put into a container of cool water that is slowly heated up, that frog would remain in the water and ultimately boil itself to death."

There were repressed sounds of shock at Reverend Meachum's pronouncement. He raised his voice a little and placed more emphasis in his tone. "Now, friends, listen to me when I tell you, when it comes to rock and roll, the same analogy applies. Our youth is that frog, and rock and roll is the water that heats up to greater and greater degrees. The term 'rock and roll' means fornication. It has been rightly described as the music of the genitals." The expressions of shock became clearly more audible as the reverend resumed his sermon. "It is a street term for sexual immorality. Rock and roll has wrecked the lives of many of our youth through immorality, perversion, drug abuse, suicide, and need I say it? Satanism!"

"Amen, Brother Todd," shouted a man, "Amen!"

He raised his voice even more, "And to our shame, we Christians and church leaders have allowed this demonic music into our homes! Where is our discernment, good people? What has happened to our sense of discretion? Are we Christians losing our ability to discern the difference between good and evil?"

"Preach on, Brother Todd!" another man shouted.

Reverend Meachum then pointed an accusatory finger at the congregation, "We are being deluged with hard rock, acid rock, psychedelic rock and satanic rock! It is invading the sanctity of our own *homes*! And we do not see the evil it has brought forth! Truly, we are the frogs! And the water is boiling – because it is being kindled by the very fires of Hell!"

"Keep it comin', Brother Todd!" exclaimed another member, "Keep it comin'!"

The Reverend then quieted his voice a little as he resumed speaking. "I had to do a lot of research in the preparation of this sermon... and I had to go to sources I normally wouldn't even touch! But this message, I felt, was so important that my distaste for the literature that gave me the information I am about to impart to you would have to be put aside so that I might fully convey to you the extent to which this evil has made inroads into our society and contributed to its immeasurable decay! And with that said, I would like to say to you that if you are a Christian and you don't realize that rock and roll is evil and demonic, then you'd better get your spiritual eyes examined, or you, my friends, are in deep trouble!"

A chill then fell over the audience.

"As I read the history of rock and roll, I observed how Satan brought in his music in the 1950s. We were still frogs in relatively cool waters, although there were some prophetic voices who dared to warn us that the waters were getting warmer. Those voices, of course, were discredited and mocked to silence by scoffers like Alan Freed and Dick Clark. The message of the music during this time might have been seen by many as harmless. The lyrics of the tunes might have promoted good times, teenage romance, cars, surfing, and new dance fads such as the twist, the hulley gulley, the popeye, the jerk, the mash potato, the watusi... all of which may have appeared innocent on the surface, but make no mistake about it... the uninhibited body motions of these new dances were just beginning to sow the seeds of sexual promiscuity, while surfing and hot-rodding and good times were sowing the seeds of rebellion in our youth, causing them to question the authority of their parents, causing them to rebel against the chores they were made to do and disrespect their parents' dominion. And I quote the words of one of these songs: 'Take out the papers and the trash, or you don't get no spending cash. If you don't scrub that kitchen floor, you ain't gonna rock and roll no more, yackety-yak, don't talk back.' Another distasteful tune of childish vulgarity: 'I boogied in the kitchen, I boogied in the hall, I boogied on my finger and I wiped it on the wall.' The list is endless, and the examples are irrefutable."

Reverend Meachum paused briefly. "So, the stage was being set at that time for the seeds of rebellion to prosper. The 'greaser' image became popular. The music would blend the big band sound with its powerful physical dance influence, with 'rhythm and blues,' based on pagan African rhythms. One of the performers, Little Richard, who later became a preacher and born-again Christian, said undeniably that this was the devil's music. He openly testified how it led him into drugs and perverted sexual activities, but he went on to say, 'It took the love of Jesus to deliver me from the sin-filled folly I was into so deep.' Another performer, Jerry Lee Lewis, the cousin of Evangelist Jimmy Swaggart, openly admitted, 'I play the devil's music and I play it well. It's got me in its grip and I just can't get loose. If I didn't play it so well, I'd be a Christian.' So if rock's own performers come out and admit that about their music, how can we Christians dare to defend it?"

At that juncture several members of the congregation said in union with one another, "Amen, Brother Todd! Amen! Amen! and Amen!"

"But let me go further, for the Lord has much to say on this topic! Look at how the music evolved during the sixties. The water is indeed getting hotter, and we dumb frogs are still in it!"

"The message of rebellion is even stronger now than it was ten years ago, and this rebellion inevitably was the thread through which all future rock was to receive its base. The lyrics of the tunes now promoted sex, drugs and rebellion against authority, and it dared to present them as harmless fun. 'Lucy in the Sky with Diamonds,' a paean to the drug LSD. 'Ridin' that train, high on cocaine,' 'Comin' down from Los Angeles, bringing in a couple of keys,' 'Help me make it through the night,' 'Society's child,' 'everybody must get stoned,' ... need I say more?"

"Say on, Brother Todd! Say on!"

"Folk groups were also present on the scene promoting anti-establishment attitudes like 'we're on the eve of destruction,' 'little play soldiers if only you knew, what kind of battles are waiting for you.' Barry McGuire was one of these anti-establishment musicians. But he came to Jesus and renounced his folly. Bob Dylan also saw the error of his ways and now sings praises to the Lord Jesus Christ! So, if these musicians can recognize their music as demonic and destructive in nature, how can we, as Christians, justify its presence in our lives? How can we dare to allow our kids to be exposed to its evil and destructive influence? And let us not forget the introduction of Satanism! The Rolling Stone's 'Sympathy for the Devil!' How much clearer can they get? How much more proof do you need?"

The congregation sat riveted to their pews.

"And now, here it is, the nineteen-seventies! We now have acid rock, hard rock, and theatrical Satanic rock! Music has developed a greater hypnotic effect, captivating its listeners and feeding them evil thoughts, while satanic messages are hidden or camouflaged by backward masking. Have you heard them? I challenge you, if you dare to abuse your stereo equipment, get one of your teenager's records out and play it backwards. I did. And let me tell you I was shocked to the marrow. 'Stairway to Heaven,' 'The Night the Electricity Went Off In Arkansas,' 'Welcome to the Hotel California' ... I guarantee what you will hear will chill you to the bone, and I'm just scratching the surface. The forward lyrics ain't much better; they further advocate no morals, the endorsement of homosexuality, no responsibilities, and distain for authority. Drugs and rock music have become synonymous. Stage violence has become the norm. There is a sharper focus on false religion. Groups are actually seen destroying their instruments on the stage. Cross-dressing and bizarre makeup have come into vogue. One example of this trend rests with the group KISS--K-I-S-S being an acronym for Kings In Satan's Service. Can I get any clearer?"

At this point, the teens in the congregation were being divided into three different camps: Those in zealous agreement, those who remained indifferent, and those who had to restrain themselves from showing their overt hostility to Reverend Meachum's pronouncements. One hefty-looking male teen, losing what little control he had, stood up and hollered, "Bull s---," but was muzzled by his father placing his hand over the youth's mouth before he could complete his sentiment.

Undaunted by the disruption, Reverend Meachum resumed, "The lyrics blatantly denounce Christianity and present the devil as the answer. Violence, sex, rebellion, and drugs are not only openly promoted, but are acted out on stage. Some lyrics even promote suicide. The music has become violent, loud and abrasive, combining the elements of disco, hard rock, and 1950s music, while its synchronization has begun to create an electronic, mechanical sound, simulating the controlling power of rock music. Thus, the rock music of today has evolved into the single most powerful tool that enables Satan to communicate his evil messages to our youth. Search your child's record collection and see what your son or daughter harbors. These theatrical Satan-rock performers include such people as KISS, Eagles, Iron Maiden, Black Sabbath, AC/DC, Judas Priest, the Grateful Dead, and Alice Cooper, to name only a few."

"My good brethren, to the Christian, God says in His word, and if you will turn with me to the apostle Paul's letter to the Ephesians, chapter 5, verse 11..."

There was fumbling through Bibles.

"'And have no fellowship with the unfruitful

works of darkness, but rather reprove them.' Again turn with me to the Book of Matthew, chapter 7, verses 18 and 20…"

Pages rustled…

"And the Lord Jesus said 'A good tree cannot bring forth evil fruit, neither can a corrupt tree bring forth good fruit. Wherefore by their fruits ye shall know them.' So, the question here is what kind of fruit does rock and roll produce? There is definitely fruit to rock and roll, and all of it is evil. I tell you, good brethren, this demonic music has been a major tool and vehicle used for the satanic popularization of such evils as drug abuse, immorality, perverted sex, blasphemy against God and sacred things, homosexuality, occultism, and Satanism. In His word, my friends, God has instructed us not to have any fellowship with the unfruitful works of darkness. Rock and roll is such a fruit."

The reverend continued, "We, as good Bible-believing Christians, have no business listening to secular rock, for it is all an abomination to God. I say to all you parents in the congregation today, if your son or daughter has brought rock and roll records into your home, he or she has brought a demon to reside in your household, a demon that can only be exorcised by fire!

"God also says in his word, and please turn with me again, dear brethren, to First John, chapter

2, verses 15 and 16 and read with me. 'Love not the world, neither the things that are in the world. If any man love the world, the love of the Father is not in him, but is of the world.'

"Now, would you turn with me to First Peter, chapter 1, verses 14 through 16, and read with me, if you will.."

Again the congregation frantically fumbled to keep up.

"'As obedient children, not fashioning yourselves according to the former lusts in your ignorance. But as He which hath called you is holy, so be ye holy in all manner of conversation; Because it is written, Be ye holy; for I am holy.'

"Now, dear brethren, turn with me again to Second Corinthians, Chapter 7, verse 1. Read with me..."

At this point people could hear a certain male parishioner mumble, "God, how many more verses does he expect us to find?"

"'With these promises clearly set before us, dearly beloved, let us cleanse ourselves: from all filthiness of the flesh and spirit, perfecting ourselves in holiness.' Perfecting ourselves in holiness – I now ask you earnestly, dear brethren, how can a satanic person be holy? We are commanded in God's word to be holy! But how can we be so when an earring is hung in the ear, sexually provocative clothes are worn, and rebellion is in vogue? It is now that I call on all you good parents: search your teenager's record collection. Weed out these demonic abominations. Set your sons and daughters free from the vile grip that Satan has placed upon them! Remove them from that broad path that leads them to destruction and return them to the narrow path of Jesus! And set your homes free from the demonic transgressions that have invaded the sanctity of home and hearth! Truly, I tell you, only fire may purge us from the grasp of Satan – and with fire, we can send this sordid abomination back into the pit of Hell where it belongs! Let us pray."

At that point, all in the congregation bowed their heads and closed their eyes, some out of reverence, some out of just pure exhaustion.

"Most merciful Heavenly Father, we call upon thee now... for to our shame, in our lack of vigilance we have reaped bitter fruit, the devil's own harvest. Grant us the courage of our convictions, sharpen our sense of vigilance, create in us a sharper sense of discernment, and strengthen our resolve that we might purge our youth, ourselves and our community of this base, demonic entity that presently thrives among us. We are weak, Father. Only in You can we find the strength to do the task You have commissioned us to do by Your will. It is for this strength we now beseech thee, 0 Lord, in the name of Jesus Christ we pray, Amen."

Reverend Meachum's sermon left an indelible mark on those in attendance that Sunday, but it did not stop just at the Victory Over Evil Christian Fellowship. Tapes of the message were circulated about the community and distributed to every church within a 200-mile radius of Georgetown County. Transcripts of Meachum's message were also circulated about the state of South Carolina, and word of its message even made news on Christian radio stations. Newspapers printed the message, and within the boundaries of Georgetown County, church and community steering committees were gathering and preparing to implement Reverend Meachum's suggestion, namely the public burning of their children's rock records.

The only church holding off in the matter was the church pastored by Reverend Elwood Piggins. Reverend Piggins harbored a good deal of ambivalence on the issue, and this uncertainty was met with astounding opposition by the church's elders and the pulpit steering committee. As they met that Wednesday evening at the church, the following conversation ensued.

"Look," said Reverend Piggins, "I'll admit a lot of it sounds like the devil, but turning us into a bunch of pyromaniacs just because of that wacko reverend over at Victory Over Evil Christian

Fellowship…"

"Reverend Piggins," Elder Joe Benson, a man in his late fifties with a slender build and a full head of jet-black hair and matching facial foliage, interjected, "have you read or listened to the Reverend Meachum's sermon?"

"I have," Elwood replied. "The sermon was very strong on the scriptural isogesis realm of interpretation, yet extremely weak in its exegesis. My studies in the discipline of homiletics have always reinforced the point that conformity to the scriptures within the settings they were written – that sitz im leben or 'settings in life,' pertaining to the period in which they originated, must be faithfully adhered to, and any meaning to be taken from that setting must be restructured to fit into the contemporary setting. I find the Reverend Meachum's sermon to be sadly lacking in that area and potentially dangerous as a result of that deficiency. You see, rock and roll was not around in the time of Jesus, at least as far as we know. True, the Jewish subculture out of which Christianity evolved was surrounded by the somewhat base Roman culture present at the time of the writings of the Synoptic Gospels, but it was a different world back then, and those differences need to be respected when presenting the scriptures in the context of a sermon. 1 realize my sermons might be a bit duller than the Reverend Meachum's, but I refuse to exchange the integrity of scriptures for the sake of sensationalism just to get a larger audience. I find such an approach to be..."

"Reverend Piggins," Michael Jurgens, another elder who was a portly, bespectacled man in his mid sixties, completely bald on top, with short, gray hair on the sides, interrupted, his voice fraught with concern, "with all due respect, did it ever occur to you that all your schooling, your seminary training, your constant reading, may have served to spiritually blind you to certain obvious dangers that are abundantly present in this community? It takes a man like the Reverend Meachum to notice and speak out on these matters! And it's up to us, as good, God-fearing Christians, to take action!"

Elwood was quick to counter Mr. Jurgens as he adamantly pointed to himself, "And it's up to me, as shepherd of this flock, to equip the saints to act circumspectly in such matters, using all the resources accorded me in the capacity of ministry. To do less would be grossly negligent on my part." Then he pointed to Mr. Jurgen, "But speaking to your issue regarding my seminary training and my ongoing education, I cannot, for the life of me, understand your disdain of it. If you were to go to a doctor, wouldn't you want to make sure this doctor was equipped with the right medical training to qualify himself as an effective physician? Wouldn't you want your doctor to have the proper credentials from an accredited medical school? Wouldn't you want your doctor to continue his reading and education so he could keep current on new discoveries in medicine as it pertained to you and your afflictions? Or would you simply trust your body to a man who loves medicine and healing but has no true background as to the nature of the healing process? If you needed a lawyer, wouldn't you want a lawyer who was schooled in the discipline of law, and was continually upgrading his knowledge regarding the new laws that have been passed in the areas of the law he practiced and the new precedents that had been set via court decisions? Or would you take your legal matters to a man who simply loves the law? The same principle holds for a minister." Elwood then pointed at the elders, "To serve you in the true capacity of God's call, I find I must draw upon the resources imparted to me from my seminary training, the seminars I attend, books and articles dealing with the church and its growth and well-being. As your minister, I cannot simply qualify myself as such by merely professing a love for the Lord. To be worthy to shepherd this flock, I must continually equip myself with ways of being more effective in my task."

There was a desperation in Elwood's voice as

he continued to justify his stance. "Reverend Meachum is a dynamic speaker and, no doubt, I cannot dispute he is a true believer. But I know the man's credentials, and he is sadly lacking. I'm sure you've often heard the old adage, 'Don't judge a book by its cover. Well, we do it all the time. Remember how in First Samuel, Samuel could not believe that out of all of Jesse's sons, it would be David, the supposedly least qualified, that God would choose to lead a nation?"

"Reverend Piggins," Michael chimed in as he straightened his posture and shifted about in his seat, "I can appreciate your sentiments, but we cannot ignore the more-than-obvious truth here! No disrespect intended, but hasn't it even affected your own household? Hasn't your own daughter gotten caught up in this frenzy? Don't you think her record collection could warrant some examination on your part?"

Elwood sighed and leaned his head against the back of his chair. "Point well taken. I will look at my daughter's collection. But please, promise me, let's not do anything hasty. We are also commanded in the scriptures to 'walk circumspectly, not as foolish men, but as wise.' And that is scripture you can apply to any age, in both its exegesis and its isogesis." The meeting drew to a close shortly after Elwood's proclamation. The elders murmured their differing sentiments and left the room with varying degrees of frustration and defeat, the last even pounding his fist on the door frame as he left.

8

As they entered the house after the elders meeting, Elwood spoke to Ellen. "You know, Ellen, I feel like something of a sneak going through Lawanda's things when she's not home."

"Well, Elwood," Ellen replied, "she hasn't exactly earned our trust, we do have a responsibility as parents to look after her best interests, and there might be something to what the Reverend Meachum had to say. So, let's be a little sneaky!"

Just then, they heard a knock at the door. Elwood opened the door, and there stood Reverend Meachum, diminutive in stature yet huge and with a presence in Elwood's mind that was supremely imposing. Having spent the better part of the elders' meeting discussing the content of Meachum's renowned sermon, Elwood certainly didn't want to see him at this time.

"Reverend Meachum!" Elwood exclaimed. "What a surprise! We spent an entire church meeting discussing your sermon and the controversy it's stirred up, and now you grace us with your presence at our doorstep. Well, don't just stand there! Come on in!"

Reverend Meachum entered the house. "I was just in the neighborhood and thought I'd drop by. Mrs. Piggins ..." he said with a nod, then turned his attention back to Elwood. "Reverend Piggins, am I to understand that you didn't like my sermon?"

Elwood addressed Reverend Meachum as the three of them moved to the center of the living room, "It's not a question of liking or not liking. I just said I had reservations about its content and about the liberties you appeared to take with the scriptures. However, I promised the elders I'd follow through with an investigation of my daughter's record collection, so that's what we are about to do right now. Would you care to join us? I mean, you might as well since you're already here and you claim it's your area of expertise."

"I'd be honored," replied Reverend Meachum, and the three of them proceeded up the stairs. "Practically everyone in the community is familiar with your daughter's exploits."

Elwood sighed as they continued their ascent, "All I can say is I've done the best I can and I'm hoping to continue to do so tonight."

Reverend Meachum was quick to counter, "Oh, I'm not criticizing you. I have some teenage children of my own... and I do use the word 'children.' I've told them time and again, 'only when I'm convinced you're adults will I see you as other than children.' I tell you, they can be stubborn as sin and twice as nasty. But God has given me authority over them, and for their own good, I will exercise that authority. They're not going to be very happy about having their record collection burned, but I don't preach something I don't practice."

"Look, Reverend," Elwood responded, "isn't the calling for a community bonfire a little extreme? I mean, it almost appears fascist by its very nature."

"Elwood, " Reverend Meachum replied, "you know as well as I do what the Good Book says about the purging of demons by fire."

"Elwood," said Ellen, "are you afraid of what Lawanda's response is going to be if her record collection is destroyed?"

Elwood sighed as his voice began to tremble, "Yes. I'm scared to death. I feel I've failed as a parent." Elwood's voice quivered and his eyes started to water.

Reverend Meachum put his hand on Elwood's shoulder. "Brother Elwood, I know you've done everything you could to be a good parent. But even the best of parents cannot hope to succeed when there are demons present, wielding their evil influence on our progeny."

Elwood turned and faced Reverend Meachum. "That's exactly what I was referring to! Demons! I'll have you know that back in seminary, I wrote an eighty-page paper on demons and demonology in the Old Testament. It was the driest topic I ever wrote about. I felt at the end of the paper that I had spent almost an eternity in the Middle Eastern deserts. In the New Testament, Jesus was called upon to cast out a demon. He stated that the only way this demon could be cast out was through prayer. A careful exegesis of the scriptures along with the utilization of form and redaction criticism revealed that this "demon" was epilepsy and the supposed seizure the man was having was construed by the ancients as 'being seized by the devil.' That's how the term 'seizure' came about."

"Now, look, Elwood," replied Reverend Meachum, "I don't have all your high falutin' seminary education…"

"Okay," said Elwood, "Try this. I also learned during one of my units of Clinical Pastoral Training that other psychiatric afflictions could also have been ascribed to demonic possession: Tourette's syndrome, schizophrenia, and shoot, I even have a cousin in Tyler, Texas, who's been diagnosed with bipolar disorder, another disorder that's been described as having seizures connected with it."

"Elwood," Ellen said, "we may know more now than the ancients did, but we still don't know everything. We need to keep our minds open to different possibilities. And we promised we would look through our daughter's collection. Best we do it before she gets home."

"Okay, fine!" Elwood stomped up the stairs as he spoke over his shoulder. "I always did want to listen to music backwards, and perhaps my ingenious colleague could lend me his expertise on the matter---not that I want to ruin expensive stereo equipment."

"Brother," Reverend Meachum responded as he followed Elwood and Ellen up the stairs, "what profits a man to keep his expensive stereo equipment and lose his daughter's everlasting soul?"

They made their way into Lawanda's room. Ellen flipped on the lights. Elwood looked about the premises. Clothing was strewn on the floor and hanging from the headboard of her bed, the bed was unmade with piles of junk resting on top of it-hair curlers, magazines, old records left out of their jackets. Her closet was in an even greater state of disarray, with more clothes on the floor, open food scattered around the room, and an assortment of empty pop bottles here and there. "My God!" Elwood exclaimed, "This room's a mess! When was the last time you had her clean it, dear?"

"Yesterday," Ellen responded embarrassed. "I guess I didn't ride herd on her enough."

"Oh, well, first things first." Elwood pointed to the far comer. "I believe those are the records we're looking for. Okay, Todd, apparently you know more about this subject than I do, so as we inventory, you point out the 'dangerous, demon-infested records' and we'll examine them." They began going through the records. "W. Lee O'Daniels and the Light Crust Dough Boys? That's my record! How'd it get in here?"

"Well," Ellen responded, "I was organizing things one day and placed all the records together in one place."

"Okay." said Elwood. "Let's see, what's next. Buck Owens and the Buckaroos?"

"That's Elmo's record, dear. He likes to watch 'Hee Haw.'"

"John Denver."

"Set that one aside, Brother!" Reverend Meachum exclaimed. "He's into drugs and eastern mysticism."

"Maybe so, but what he does in his personal life's really no concern of mine. Even Frank Sinatra, I'm told, snorted a little coke."

"But his songs even advocate drug use!"

"Really? How so?"

"Colorado Rocky Mountain High, with the emphasis on 'high.'"

"That's a bit of a stretch don't you think? Besides, wasn't he the one who replaced Chad Mitchell in the Mitchell Trio?"

"I don't know about that, but he's got a cult-like following now and his songs are laced heavily with counterfeit spirituality. Listen sometime to the words of his song 'Gospel Changes.' Jesus didn't lay down to die. He was crucified, Brother."

"Okay, so he was ignorant about how the Lord died. I'm sure you are acutely aware of the widespread ignorance among the laity. But I'll set it aside and give it some consideration." And Elwood reached for the next record. "Okay! Pay dirt! Here's the record with 'Stairway to Heaven' on it. All right, Reverend! Play it! I'm anxious to hear this back-masked message! I'm also anxious to see how you make the turntable go backwards."

"No trick to it," Reverend Meachum replied. "You place the turntable indicator between speeds and turn it manually until it replicates the sound played at its normal speed, more or less." Reverend Meachum proceeded to turn the stereo on and manually manipulate the turntable.

The sound materialized. It was a gruesome, abrasive sound that spoke undeniably, "Here's to my sweet Satan... the one whose little path would make me sad, whose power is fake/Satan. He'll give those with him 666. There was a little tool shed where he made us suffer, sad Satan."

"My God!" exclaimed Elwood. "No doubt, that record's definitely going to the dump!"

"No, Brother!" Reverend Meachum retorted. "Save it for the fire!"

"The dump also burns garbage, and in a safely contained area. And if you'll recall in the scriptures, a metaphor for Hell was Gehena, Jerusalem's city dump. It was always on fire. However, because of the air-quality standards we have in place here in Georgetown County, we can't have a fire going constantly uncontained outdoors."

"But you see, Brother, this fire has a two-fold purpose. All the churches are gathering together, and everyone is to bring their children along. We are going to pray in groups and singularly for a reversal of the demonization that has taken place with our youth!"

"A fire and an exorcism. That sounds too macabre for me."

"Dear," said Ellen, frustrated by her husband's nitpicking. "we still have several records to go through."

"Okay," replied Elwood as he picked up another record, "Eagles, 'Hotel California.'"

Reverend Meachum took the album from Elwood. "Definite Satanic inspiration. See that picture in the comer?" Reverend Meachum said pointing to the upper right-hand comer of the album."

"Yeah," Elwood responded. "What about it?"

"That's a picture of Alistair Crowley, prominent Satanist of the nineteenth and early twentieth century. He was the one who inspired the back-masking. He practiced doing everything backwards... talking backwards, and even walking backwards."

"Sounds like a kook."

"Our youth and their pop singers are idolizing that 'kook.' And the lyrics of the song 'Hotel California' ... one line, 'you can check out any time you like, but you can never leave.' That's a reference to the Remington Spa that Mr. Crowley put a curse on. This curse doomed all the residents, past, present, and future, to return to the spa after their time on this plane had expired. Thus, according to legend, the Remington Spa was to serve as the devil's gathering ground for condemned souls. And even when the residents of the spa checked out, they could never truly leave because, according to the myth of Satanic doctrine, once the devil lays claim on your soul, you can never truly break free."

"Dump," said Elwood.

"No," Reverend Meachum replied, "fire."

"I'm inclined to agree with Reverend Meachum, dear," Ellen said.

Elwood sighed, "All right. Fine. But I'm still not convinced I should lend my endorsement to this activity."

"Well, Brother," Reverend Meachum replied, "we still have more records to go through."

And go through them they did, examining all aspects of each record, from the drawings on the cover, to the forward lyrics, to the back-masked messages. Finally Elwood conceded, "I'm beginning to get the picture. I've never heard anything more vulgar, more repugnant! Is there any evidence this form of subliminal messaging can wield influence on the human psyche?"

"Is there any evidence it cannot? Would you like to hear more?" Another hour passed. Message after message drummed out its repellent espousal of evil. Elwood and Ellen stood transfixed between stark horror and acute nausea. Near the end of what appeared to be an immeasurable interval of torture, Elwood and Ellen had weeded out four-fifths of Lawanda's record collection.

"Here!" Elwood exclaimed, handing the records over to Reverend Meachum. "Take them! Burn them! Just get them out of my home, out of my sight! I just can't believe anything so awful could be allowed to be produced, to be sold, to be even allowed to exist!"

"Then your eyes have been opened, Brother?"

"Opened? I don't think I'll be able to sleep tonight! This is enough to make me start believing in the bogeyman again!"

"Before I leave, we'll say a prayer for sleep."

A noise was then heard from downstairs. "It's Lawanda!" Ellen whispered.

"Oh, my God!" Elwood exclaimed. "If she finds out what we're doing, all hell's going to break loose!"

"Brother Piggins," said Reverend Meachum, looking sternly into Elwood's eyes, "we are doing the Lord's work here tonight! For that, no apology or excuse needs to be offered. You are exercising the divine stewardship God has commissioned for you over your family. And for that reason, God is now watching over you. So, out of faith, He now charges you to confront this situation, your daughter, and this present evil and the power it has wrought over her squarely in the face."

"You're right!" Elwood responded, heading for the stairs, "How I could let this garbage into my house in the first place…?"

Before Elwood could complete his sentence, Lawanda's eyes had ascended the staircase. Her hair appeared disheveled, her makeup smudged. She was wearing blue-jean cutoffs and a brown halter top. Adorned about her neck were beads and a necklace. On her head she wore a red bandana. She looked upward and fixed her eyes upon Reverend Meachum, her mother, and her father coming out of her room. Her eyes almost instantly lit upon her father carrying what she recognized to be an armful of her records. "Give me my records!" She screamed as she rushed to forcibly take them from her father's grasp.

Elwood swung the records out of Lawanda's reach. "We're going to burn them, dear." Was her father's stoic answer.

"Over my dead body!"

Ellen reached for her daughter and embraced her in a conciliatory fashion and spoke to her in a voice that was soft, warm, and loving. "Dear, we're doing this because we love you and want the best for you. We want God's best for you. Are you aware of what's on these records? Have you heard the horrible back-masked messages?"

Lawanda winced in response to her mother's query. A bolt of rage swept through her, engulfing the very core of her being. She clenched her teeth as her face contorted and her voice metamorphosed into a chilling snarl. "Give me back my records! You have no right to take them!" she screamed.

Reverend Meachum then placed his hand firmly upon Elwood's shoulder. "Hold tight, Brother!" He uttered. "The devil's surely got a foothold here!"

Lawanda then stepped back to the foot of the staircase, pointed accusingly at the Reverend Meachum, and screamed vehemently, "You! You're the one who's garbage they listened to! You're the one who's brainwashed everybody in this town! My band lost two gigs this week, because of you!"

"Now, listen here, young lady," Reverend Meachum countered, "your parents are doing this out of love, and you need to respect that!"

Lawanda kicked Reverend Meachum in the left shin. Reverend Meachum let out a yell and reached for the spot Lawanda had kicked. It was then that they heard another noise from downstairs. It was Elmo. "What's going on up there?" Elmo asked.

Lawanda screamed, "Mom and Dad are burning my records!"

"What about mine?" Elmo charged up the stairs. "Do I still get to keep my Buck Owens and Glen Campbell?"

"Go look for yourself," Ellen said, then noticed adorned about Lawanda's neck a necklace with a strange design. "What kind of necklace is this?"

"It's an upside down pentagram!" The Reverend Meachum exclaimed as he peered over Ellen's shoulder. "It's a mark of Satan!"

Elwood grabbed the necklace and said emphatically, "This has got to go."

"No way!" Lawanda shouted. "It's mine!"

"Don't argue with me, Lawanda!" Elwood had fire in his eyes now. "It's coming off!" And he yanked the necklace off Lawanda's neck.

"Hey," Lawanda shouted, "give it back!"

"Lawanda," Ellen spoke, "we're doing this for your own good."

"Fuck you!" Lawanda cried. "Fuck you all! I hope you all burn in Hell!" And with that Lawanda rushed out the door and into the night.

"Shades of Linda Blair!" Elwood exclaimed.

"Man!" Elmo cried, watching as the door slammed behind her. "I've never seen her this mad before!"

"You definitely have a problem, Brother!" said Reverend Meachum. "I'll help you look for her, though."

Elwood started to tremble, and his eyes began to water.

"Elwood?" Ellen said as she embraced her husband.

Elwood's voice trembled. "I've lost control of this house!" He began to weep.

Elmo spoke up. "Well, for what it's worth, Daddy, I still love you. You may be nasty at times and make me do things I don't want to do, but I guess that's all part of having parents."

Elwood tearfully placed his hand on young Elmo's shoulder.

Reverend Meachum placed his hand on Elwood's shoulder. "Well, it's obvious that you've done something right with this young man here."

"I hope the same can be said when he reaches adolescence," Ellen shot back.

"Brother," Reverend Meachum continued, "it's times like these, when the Lord senses our brokenness, that He truly can use us. Let's all gather in prayer, then we'll go out and find your daughter."

They all gathered in a circle, bowed their heads and prayed. Young Elmo wasn't sure what was going on, but as usual, he took it all in.

9

The search lasted until four in the morning, when they lumbered wearily homeward. Elwood had notified the police during the course of the search, but the police informed him that the person had to be missing for at least twenty-four hours before they could put out an all-points bulletin.

As they entered the house, Elwood spoke to Reverend Meachum, "What you said about God using my brokenness? Well, I sure don't feel very useful now."

They heard a shuffling noise in the kitchen. Ellen and Elwood rushed toward the kitchen, and there sat Lawanda having a bite to eat. "Lawanda! What's the idea of scaring your mother and me like that?" Elwood yelled even as he collapsed in relief into a kitchen chair.

"A lot you care!" Lawanda yelled back.

"Of course, I care! Why do you think I'm yelling at you like I am? I wouldn't be this angry, if I didn't care!"

"I hate you!"

Elwood nearly buckled at Lawanda's words, like he had been struck below the belt. "You hate me?" he said in an almost expressionless tone. "Well let me tell you something, young lady, you don't have to earn my love, because you're my daughter and I'm going to love you no matter what. It's late, I'm tired, so I'm going to bed." He then turned to Reverend Meachum, "Reverend Meachum, forgive my lack of manners. Thank you for all you've done for us tonight. I'd thank you in a more proper manner were I not so exhausted." He then walked toward Ellen and placed his hand on her cheek, "Good night, honey." Elwood marched wearily up the stairs to the master bedroom.

Reverend Meachum turned to Lawanda and said, "Young lady, never doubt what your father said to you tonight. He does love you. He loves you indeed. And he proved it tonight, putting your interest above his own." He then faced Ellen. "Mrs. Piggins, we'll see you this Sunday at the community record burning?"

"Yes. And don't forget the records." She headed back to the living room to retrieve the stack of records.

"No!" Lawanda screamed as she realized her collection could still be rescued. Ellen held Lawanda back with one hand as she handed the records to Reverend Meachum with the other. Reverend Meachum took the stack from Ellen and continued out the door in one motion. Lawanda tried to go after him but Ellen restrained her.

"Lawanda," she said, "this is for your own good! You'll thank us for this one day!"

Lawanda's psyche reeled about in fury at her mother's pronouncement. "When Hell freezes over, I'll thank you!" Lawanda's voice was thick with ferocity.

"That's enough, young lady," Ellen said with great resolve. Her patience was wearing thin with her rebellious daughter and fatigue was setting in. "You still have school today. It's three hours until time for you to be getting up and you haven't even been to bed yet. So get some rest while you still can."

Begrudgingly, Lawanda climbed the staircase and headed for her room.

Ellen then turned to her son. "Elmo, the same holds true for you."

"Yes, Mother." Elmo replied and then hurriedly rushed up the staircase to his room. Ellen heaved a sigh. "Heaven help us. Heaven help us all."

10

Morning came too early for the Piggins household. For Elmo and Lawanda, school began at eight. Elwood needed to be down at the church by nine to finish up some administrative matters and make connections with the elders about the decision to participate in the coming Sunday's community record burning. Each pastor was to either take part in a reading of scripture, a prayer, or related liturgy. Elwood still had mixed feelings regarding his involvement with the process, so he felt a further conference with the elders was in order before he could lend his full endorsement to the church's involvement in the event.

Morning passed. Elwood partook of more than his fair share of coffee during those hours just to maintain a modicum of alertness while he tended to his ministerial functions.

Meanwhile, Lawanda's resentment and feelings of violation were enhanced all the more by the removal of her records and her necklace, and even her other means of adornment that were called into suspect. She began to feel further deprivation of her emerging sense of autonomy. She resurrected and nursed old feelings that her identity should be exclusively her own, unique, and separate from the identity imposed upon her by her father's shadow.

Lawanda Piggins: Preacher's Daughter. From the moment of her first conscious thought, she remembered abhorring the stigma that accompanied that label. All her life, she remembered trying in desperation to free herself from its oppressive expectations. Each effort was rendered vain by the intercession of her parents, and at times, her communal surroundings. Today was no exception.

As she sat in class, fatigue overtaking her, sharp feelings of despondency began to overwhelm her. Freedom, she thought, always beyond my reach... beckoning, teasing. Resignation swept over her as a sense of depression lay claim upon her soul.

Elwood and Ellen shared Lawanda's feelings of exhaustion. Yet the luxury of slumber could not be accorded them. They still needed to tend to supper, if not for the two of them, at least for young Elmo.

"Elwood," said Ellen, "I don't really feel like cooking tonight. Why don't we just phone out for a pizza?"

"Better make it two," Elwood replied. "That way, if Lawanda changes her mind and decides to eat, there'll be some for her."

The evening passed peacefully. Ellen wrapped the leftover slices in plastic and placed them in the refrigerator for Lawanda to heat up at a later time. Finally it was time for sleep, a welcome end to the tumult of the day.

11

The rest of the week passed. Elwood reluctantly lent his endorsement to the community record burning. The elders and the church board, caught up in the spasms of enthusiasm and great anticipation, were quick to act upon his endorsement. Elwood had to coordinate with Reverend Meachum and Pastor Michael Davis, the minister of the local Holy Roller Brethren Church, regarding his role in the liturgical process of the event.

The much-anticipated Sunday soon dawned upon Georgetown County. Parents anxiously readied their children for attendance at the event. Some of the Georgetown County youth welcomed it, some resisted it mightily.

For the Piggins family, there was little doubt how the children felt. None of Elmo's records were to be burned, so he remained compliant in the matter. Lawanda, on the other hand, whose spirit of rebellion was awakened and recharged to an even greater intensity, resisted attending the event with antipathy so extreme that the devil himself would beg for reprieve. "No!" She screamed. "I will not attend your horrid old record burning! I will not subject myself to this base humiliation!"

"Lawanda!" Elwood replied. "You are coming to the event with us, and that's it! Now get upstairs, put on your white dress, comb your hair, and make yourself presentable! You have half an hour!"

"No!" she screamed.

"Lawanda," Elwood warned with a hand on his belt, "don't make this difficult."

"Do as your father says," Ellen said. Her voice was firm and resolute both in tone and deliberation. "We haven't got that much time."

Knowing herself to be sufficiently outnumbered and left with no recourse, Lawanda ascended the staircase to her room to ready herself. "Damn your souls!" she whispered under her breath.

Elwood turned to his wife as they re-entered the kitchen. "I sure hope I did the right thing endorsing this record burning. I mean, I know those records were horrible beyond my wildest imaginings, but to have a community burning... the whole idea reeks like the Spanish Inquisition, the atrocities committed during the One-hundred Years War, or even the revival of certain pagan rituals like the Festival of the Hal Dane. Shoot, for that matter, remember back in Nazi Germany when they had the book burnings?"

"Elwood," Ellen replied, "there are times when all we have to go by is our own judgment. You weighed the pros and cons out as carefully as you could... perhaps with even greater deliberation and discernment than anybody else in this county. Knowing that, you ought to be fully confident in the choice you made. You drew the conclusion that participation was the right course of action. And I stand with you and the decision you made, and harbor no feelings of reservation about it. I have no doubt the Lord will bless you in your efforts."

"I wish I was as sure of that as you. I've had a knot in my stomach about this event ever since I lent my endorsement to it. Lawanda, she's as volatile as a powder keg. I'm afraid of what she might do. I feel a profound sense of failure as a parent. And furthermore, I didn't come to any hard and fast conclusion. It was more like I yielded to the constraints of time and ..."

"Hush, dear," Ellen replied, cupping her hand on Elwood's cheek. "We must both be strong for Lawanda's sake, and for Elmo's too."

12

Elwood Piggins and family arrived at the scene of the burning early as the crowd continued to grow. The event was taking place in a large grassy field devoid of trees, yet filled with the usual infestation of ticks and chiggers common to the area. The day was slowly starting to heat up, and high humidity was already present. Mosquitoes would inevitably follow. People from all over Georgetown County and some from outside the area were arriving at the event. Members of the press were even showing up. Elwood saw television cameras positioned at various spots around the field. "Looks like this event's going to be televised," he said to Ellen.

A cleared spot of ground had been prepared for the burning. A brass ensemble was gathered in front of the crowd that had already grown to a few hundred, leading the people in the hymn, "Victory In Jesus." Elwood looked through the crowd and noted a handful of reporters with microphones seeking out comments from individuals. One stepped up and put a microphone in Elwood's face.

"Excuse me, sir," the reporter said, "are you the Reverend Elwood Piggins of the Georgetown

County Community Church?"

"Yes I am," Elwood replied.

"Aren't you the one who took a necklace away from his daughter, because you thought it was a satanic emblem?"

Elwood glanced over at Lawanda. Lawanda couldn't suppress a coy, mischievous grin.

"No comment," Elwood replied. He then turned toward his wife. "Wait here. I see Reverend Meachum. I have to speak with him." He rushed away from the reporter who appeared quite disgruntled over Elwood's abrupt dismissal and hurried over to Reverend Meachum. "Hey, Todd!" he said, "What're all these press people doing here?"

"Somebody must've notified them," Reverend Meachum replied. "That's okay! This is all for God's glory and Satan's shame! Nothing to fear when we're in the right!"

Just then a tall man that towered over Elwood like the Incredible Hulk in a conservative gray suit and black tie stepped up to the two ministers with microphone in hand. "Excuse me," he said in a dry yet forceful tone, "which one of you is the instigator of this event?"

"I am," Reverend Meachum replied.

"I'm Russell Tiberon of KUBS network. Is it true that you're violating the rights of these children, interfering with their freedom of expression and unjustly imposing censorship and your brand of morality on them?"

"Sir," Reverend Meaqchum replied, as he pointed his finger into the camera, "I'll have you know that these are our children! We have been commissioned by God Almighty as stewards over our children. Today, we are exercising that stewardship as the Lord has so commanded! To do less would condemn us for the sin of negligence! Out children brought these records, complete with their demonic messages, into our homes! They most likely purchased them with our money, for which we labored honestly, and we reserve the right to burn these objects of Satan—for the acknowledgment of God's sovereignty, the betterment of this community, and the uplifted quality of life for our youth! As for our children's rights, that is to be left to the judgment of each of these good Christian parents here, and we do not welcome you commie interlopers from your TV network coming in and making judgments about what we can and cannot do!" As he spoke, his voice grew increasingly louder, and onlookers began to gather into a small but growing audience.

Russell Tiberon turned toward Elwood. "Reverend Piggins, I understand you forced your daughter to get rid of a necklace, because you thought it was an emblem of Satan?"

"Sir," Elwood replied, "with all due respect, that is a family matter and I don't believe that's any of your business."

"Reverend Piggins..."

Reverend Meachum stepped up to Russell Tiberon and spoke, with a sideways glance at the crowd. "That necklace, Mr. Commie Network Man, happened to be an upside-down pentagram—clearly an emblem of the Devil! Now I don't know what you call it, Mr. Commie Network Man, but out here, we don't much care for letting our children be fodder for Satan, leaving them open to burn in the Devil's fires of perdition! And we're all here because we glory in God's majesty, we love our children, and we mean to give the Devil his due!"

Reverend Meachum stepped over to the microphone that had just been set up and yelled loudly into the crowd, "Friends, we have a Yankee TV network man here from KUBS network! He's here to denigrate us for what we're doing today for our young 'uns! Well, we don't harbor him no malice! We figure the Devil's gotten deep into his way of thinking! So, let's love that Devil out of him! Let's lift up our voices again in praise to the Lord." And with that, he sang thunderously into the microphone and the people joined in, "O victory in Jesus, my Savior forever, He sought me and bought me with his redeeming blood... "

Russell Tiberon turned to Elwood, "You have not heard the last of this! We will be back!"

"We'll be here," Elwood replied, and walked back to his family. He led them to the front of the crowd and went to stand with his fellow ministers and two priests. After the singing had subsided and there was silence amid the crowd, Elwood stepped up to the microphone and delivered the invocation. "Let us pray. Heavenly Father, it is Your guidance we seek this hour as we act in accordance to Your will and mandates. Our perceptions are flawed. It is through You that we seek clarity. Our motives may reflect bias. It is through You that we seek the true path of righteousness and genuine virtue. Our vision may be blurred. It is through You that we seek proper illumination of the truth that you render in Your word. Clearly, we ask all these things as we seek Your will this hour in the name of our Lord Jesus Christ, Amen." Then Elwood stepped down.

The crowd echoed with numerous "Amens" and there were quiet rumblings among those in attendance.

A petite blond girl, just barely in her teens, mounted the podium with tambourine in hand. With the drums, bass guitar, and brass ensemble, she began to perform the Wayne Rainy song, *We Need a Whole Lot More of Jesus and a Lot Less Rock 'n Roll.*

13

Pastor Michael Davis was a chubby, balding man in his early sixties. Like his colleague Todd Meachum, he was short on stature but long on charisma and gifted in oratory. With slow deliberation in his step, Pastor Davis mounted the podium and spoke loudly into the microphone, his voice reverberating from the loudspeakers. "Good Christian brethren, ladies and gentlemen, members of the press, truly I feel the powerful presence of God here with us today! Do I hear an Amen?"

The crowd shouted an exuberant "Amen!"

"Yes, friends, truly we're here for God's glory! Amen?"

Again the crowd shouted "Amen!"

"We're here today, because we love God and we love our children! Amen?"

"Amen!"

"You'd better believe Amen! We're here today, because we believe our children are gifts from God! We're here today, because God has called each of us to be stewards over these gifts! We're here today to tell Satan that these are *our* children, and they belong to God and he can't have them! Do I hear an

Amen?"

"Amen!" the crowd roared.

Then Reverend Davis pointed to his left and shouted, "Over there, our good brethren are preparing the fire we are about to feed! Today is the day we are all gathered to perform a sacred task! We are going to burn these abominable records, these spawns of Satan! We are going to send this perfidious stuff that has the audacity to pass itself off as music back into the pit of Hell where it belongs! Do I hear an Amen?"

"Amen!"

"Do I hear another Amen?"

"Amen!"

"And another!"

"Amen!" And the crowd worked itself up into a frenzy as the Reverend Davis began leading them in glossolalia.

"0h le alle akum!" was the chant that was delivered again and again as the major portion of the crowd lifted their hands.

While all this was taking place, Elmo tugged at his father's sleeve. "Daddy, what's that man saying?"

"That's glossolalia," Elwood answered. "That's the speaking in unknown tongues. It's what the people allegedly did during the time of Pentecost found in the Book of Acts."

"Can you do that, Daddy?"

"No."

These impressions would render their profound effect upon Elmo.

The prayers went on in an incessant drone as the flames grew hotter. Many of the youth stood passively as their parents prayed. Some kept attitudes of dutiful reverence and obedience. Others kept quiet, enduring the ritual, clearly wishing it would soon be over. The heat from the flames drew sweat from the pores of those in front.

Pastor Michael Davis proved himself more dynamic than the Reverend Meachum in the delivery of his oration. As the records fed the fire, parents placed their hands upon their children and prayed, many in tongues. Prayers were offered up: "Most Merciful Father, free my child from the demonic grip of Satan and lead him back to the true path of Jesus. Oh li oh li okum, ah li 0 gib li 0 gosh. Lift up the shroud of darkness, let him walk once again in Your true light."

Lawanda stood amid the crowd of parents with many firm hands placed on her head and both her shoulders. From a distance, she too could feel the heat from the fire stinging her face, making it warmer with each passing moment. Yet she remained motionless as those about her held her in place and continued to pray. The crowd droned on with prayers of intercession. With each murmur she took in and each drop of sweat that poured from her brow, a mounting sense of disquietude coupled with a growing degree of agitation and anger welled up inside her for what she was being forced to observe and endure. Finally, it could be contained no longer and sought release in a volatile explosion of rage. With a loud shriek and a sudden rush of adrenalin, she pushed her way through the crowd. "No!" she screamed. "Quit burning our records!"

The television cameras homed in as she rushed toward the fire. Elwood and a few other parents scurried after her. Scant seconds went by as other youths followed suit. The chaos that ensued became an insurmountable obstacle to the otherwise orderly progress of the record-burning ceremony. Elwood found himself knocked to the ground and trampled as parents stampeded over the field trying to round up their rebellious adolescents.

Looking up from the ground, he caught fleeting glimpses of Lawanda standing one hundred yards away. She glared back at the crowd and shouted, "That's it! No more! I'm leaving! And I'll never set foot in church again as long as I live!" She turned and rushed away through the parked cars at the edge of the clearing.

"Lawanda!" Elwood called. "Lawanda, come back!" He staggered to his feet, but was unable to make his legs run after her. The pain caused by the trampling produced a limp in his gait. He called again. "Lawanda! Please!" His voice grew quiet as despair gripped at his heart and tears filled his eyes. "Lawanda," he sobbed, "what have I done?"

The crowd scurried about, leaving Elwood unnoticed, sinking to his knees.

14

Hours later Ellen, Elwood, and Elmo arrived home. They knew they would probably see themselves on the evening news, but that was an item of secondary importance. The foremost issue on all their minds was Lawanda's disappearance. As they entered the front door the first cry from Elwood's lips was, "Lawanda?"

"Lawanda," Ellen hollered. "Answer your father."

"I have to know!" Elwood cried. "I've never been so scared in all my life, but I have to know what happened to Lawanda!"

Oblivious to the pain in his leg, he rushed up the staircase to Lawanda's room, followed closely by Ellen and Elmo. They entered her room and found her closet and drawers emptied of all her clothes. Her guitar was missing, too. Lawanda had left a note on her pillow that read as follows: "Have left for greener pastures. You've all done a great job showing me Hell. Lawanda."

Elwood's hand began to tremble. He turned to Ellen. "She left! We need to notify the police!" They did, only to be reminded that police required a more than twenty-four hour period to elapse before actions could be taken.

They watched the news that night. It came as no surprise to Elwood that the coverage of the event was slanted in opposition to the episode and was likened to a Nazi book-burning and the Salem witch trials. Russell Tiberon was the commentator, and he had plenty to say.

"It was the most barbaric spectacle I've ever had the displeasure to watch," he began. "And those ministers -- Todd Meachum and Elwood Piggins in particular -- if that's an example of Christianity in action, then I think it's time we Americans had a hard look at what freedom of religion is. There are certain religions that are, by their very nature, dangerous and harmful to the general well-being of the populace-at-large, and they prey on the darkest part of the human psyche. In our constitution, we are guaranteed freedom of religion. Perhaps the constitution should be amended to read freedom from certain religions, and based on what I saw today, there's no doubt in my mind, Christianity is one of those religions."

Elwood clicked off the television. "Bastard!" he muttered. The phone rang. Elwood answered. "Hello."

"Hello, Todd here," said Reverend Meachum. "You see the news just now?"

"Yes, I saw."

"Your daughter really stirred up a hornet's nest today and gave Mr. Newsman there a lot of ammunition!"

"My daughter's gone," Elwood replied.

"I'm sorry. I'll be praying for you, Brother."

"Pray for us all, Todd. I've a feeling there will be more to come after this."

Twenty-four hours elapsed. No word. The all-points bulletin was posted. A week went by. Still no word. The entire community had, by now, become aware of the Piggins family plight and prayers were delivered for the family by all the churches in Georgetown County. Cards of encouragement and condolences were sent out to Elwood and family.

Another week went by and still nothing to report. Ellen's and Elwood's worries and concerns were beginning to mount at an ever-increasing rate. Where was their daughter? Where was she staying? How was she eating? Was she walking the streets of some distant city? Was she lying dead in some God-forsaken field? Elwood grew more and more tense on the inside. He tried to appear as someone in control and was partly successful in doing so when it came to the performance of his ministerial duties. Yet, at the end of the day he would oftentimes head for home and break down and cry.

Near the end of that week, Todd Meachum paid

call upon Elwood at his home. "You're not the only parent whose suffered as a result of the record burning," Todd said.

There was great conviction in his voice. "For many of us, our relations with our teens won't ever be the same. Nobody said doing the Lord's will would be easy. In fact, I remember a saying that just might be suitable in this instance. It goes like this; 'Christianity is no playground. It's a battleground."

"Yeah," Elwood replied. His voice was wrought with cynicism. "And right now, I feel like one of the casualties."

"The Lord's just testing you, Brother! He's testing us all! Be strong! I'm gonna pray for you now!"

15

Over a year passed, and still no word about Lawanda. Even though they prayed for her daily, Elwood and Ellen were coming to a low ebb in the way of hope. Elmo had just turned eleven. One day, he rushed in through the kitchen door while Elwood was under the sink tinkering with the garbage-disposal unit. "Hey, Dad!" he yelled.

Elwood became startled, banging his forehead against the pipes. "Owww!" he cried as he crawled out from under the sink and rose to his feet. Still stroking his forehead, he looked down at his son holding a long-playing record album. "What do you want?" he asked.

Elmo looked up at his dad all bright-eyed, and said, "Billy lent me his Crosby, Stills, Nash and Young album! Is this an okay album to listen to?"

"How would I know?" Elwood said.

"But dad, you said we needed to be discerning about what we listen to."

"I did say that, didn't I?" Elwood then motioned toward the staircase. "Go on up to your room and play your record."

At his father's bidding Elmo rushed up the

stairs to his room.

"And keep the volume down!" Elwood hollered.

That evening, while gathered around the TV watching "Nashville Skyline," Ellen, Elwood, and Elmo heard the MC announce the following new act: "And now, straight from the heart of bayou country, the hottest new country sensation that's sweeping the nation, Lawanda Paget and The Jambalaya Five Piece Band." The camera focused on the group, and then on the young singer in the foreground, smiling effervescently, projecting with a luminescence that appeared to rival the brightest of heavenly bodies, singing her heart out for the scores of people gathered in the audience that evening.

Ellen and Elwood gazed with eyes transfixed on the image transmitted by the screen. Elmo was the first to shout, "Hey, that's Lawanda!" Ellen and Elwood looked at each other and tears came to their eyes. There could be no doubt. It was Lawanda.

The next morning, Ellen and Elwood were quick to head to the local record store and purchase Lawanda's record album. They bought several copies.

The months passed. Ellen and Elwood played their daughter's record incessantly, until it wore out. When this happened, they would rush back to the record store and buy more copies. Lawanda's songs were principally country with a little rock thrown in. Most of the songs were Lawanda's own compositions, a few they remembered her playing around the house. Discovering this, Ellen turned to Elwood with tears in her eyes and said, "Her music would sometimes grate on my nerves when she played around the house, but right now, I swear I've never heard anything sweeter."

"Me neither," Elwood responded.

Ellen and Elwood also took to scouring the newsstands each day looking for articles pertaining to this new singing sensation. Like obsessive fans they would cut out articles and make scrapbooks, volumes upon volumes, tracing their daughter's career, how she was discovered, where she was planning her next engagement, where she was residing. It was all Lawanda -- their daughter. In her own way, she had come back home to them.

16

Meantime, Elmo was fast approaching manhood. He was typical of the teens in the Georgetown area. He could often be seen frolicking on the beach with his friends, bodysurfing, and lying in the sun. Despite his less-than-striking appearance, Elmo also enjoyed a few intimate encounters with some of his female classmates. One in particular was Julie Welton; her father was a deacon in Elmo's church. She was a sprightly girl of fifteen, with black shoulder-length hair and brown eyes. She hadn't quite reached her full growth, but to Elmo, she looked really good in a bikini, which is what she liked to wear when she went to the beach. And the effect she had on young Elmo was made painfully obvious even when he was wearing baggy cutoffs. Julie thought it was cute. His mother was perhaps the first to notice and would express her concerns about it to Elwood. As she put it, "That boy is just one big walking hormone."

Elmo and Julie went often to the beach, choosing a remote spot where they were usually alone. One day, while bodysurfing, a strong wave tumbled them together in the sand, with his body on top of hers as the waves and seaweed rolled over them. It was like a scene in From Here to Eternity. Julie looked at Elmo and giggled. Then, without planning to and just in the spirit of fun, she planted a quick kiss on his lips. It was then that she discovered that one was not enough and went back for seconds, the second one being quite prolonged.

As the kissing progressed, both Elmo and Julie found their hands wandering across each other's bodies. Julie then decided upon a bold move and reached down into Elmo's baggies, grabbing firmly the throbbing entity that comprised his manhood.

Julie grinned mischievously and giggled, "It's big... and hard." Elmo shook all over. The next thing he found himself doing was unfastening Julie's top. After removing her top he threw it to one side. Julie's expression turned intense and she pulled Elmo close, entreating him to some hard, wet kisses, exploring his mouth with her tongue, all the while aching for him and trying to pull off his baggies. Minutes later found them both sans clothing, making passionate love on the sand as the waves continued to roll over them. A few minutes, and a climax later Elmo found his release inside her and they lay in each other's arms panting and giggling, oblivious to all of the consequences that were to follow.

A few weeks and many sand-flea bites later, Julie and Elmo met at the soda shop downtown.

Julie had phoned him and told him she had something important to tell him. After they had taken a seat in a booth, Julie disclosed the news. "Elmo," she said, looking deeply troubled, "I'm late."

"You're what?"

"I'm late."

"Well, gosh, Julie, what are you going to do?"

"Well, Elmo, I think we might have to get married."

"Married? Like, you and me?"

Julie nodded her head.

"Well, how do we go about doin' that?"

"Well, I guess first we gotta tell our folks."

"Gosh, Julie, my dad'll kill me if word of this ever leaks out!"

"What do you think my father'll do!?"

"Aw, Julie, he wouldn't do anything to you."

"No, but he will kill you."

Friday night, the Weltons invited the Piggins family over for dinner. The deacons of the church periodically had the minister and his family over for dinner. Tonight that privilege belonged to the Weltons. Mrs. Welton, a perky, slender woman like her daughter Julie, only twenty years older, would go all out for the occasion. Along with the preparation of chicken, dumplings, black-eyed peas, green beans, yellow gravy, and carrot cake, she made a beautiful magnolia centerpiece to accentuate the table decor.

Mr. Welton, a tall, slender man of thirty-nine, along with five-year-old Billy Bob, a boy with dark curly hair who was somewhat big for his age -- helped to tidy up around the house, particularly in the living room. It wasn't every day they entertained the pastor and his wife, and the family felt that a proper façade needed to be maintained.

Entertaining the pastor was right on par with entertaining Jesus himself. Just as dinner was ready, Mr. Welton heard the doorbell ring. It was the Reverend Piggins, Mrs. Piggins, and Elmo. Warm greetings and happy, jubilant banter were exchanged by all, except Elmo and Julie, who appeared somewhat withdrawn. Mr. Welton gave the matter a passing notice, but was quick to dismiss it as a phase they were going through. Teenagers, he thought, who can figure them?

Mrs. Welton then brought the food to the dining room table, and everyone gathered about their places. They remained standing as Mr. Welton said the blessing. It was a long blessing. After proper homage to God was paid with interest, everyone present assumed their seats and started passing the food around. Elwood was the first to speak, addressing Mr. Welton, "Rumor has it you're going to be opening up a new hardware store at the other end of town."

"Yes," Mr. Welton replied, "demand for hardware seems high here in Georgetown, so I figure it to be a worthwhile venture."

"Well," Ellen broke in, "we might be in need of your services, too. I've been after Elwood for I don't know how long to build a tool shed. I keep telling him the garage just isn't big enough to store all those tools he's been collecting over the years."

"I didn't know you knew how to build things, Elwood," Mrs. Welton said with surprise in her voice.

"Oh, yes," Elwood replied, "I dabble in it. But unlike Jesus, it's just a hobby for me."

"Oh, don't be so modest, Elwood," Ellen chimed in, "you've got real ability." Then she turned toward Mrs. Welton. "You know that birdbath out in our front yard?"

"Yes," Mrs. Welton replied, "that is the most darling thing! I've been meaning to ask you where you bought it. I want to get one for our yard."

"Elwood made it."

"No!"

"From materials he purchased from your husband's store."

Elwood blushed a little.

"Tell me," Mrs. Welton said addressing Ellen, "you think you could convince him to build one for us?"

"I can ask him. Elwood..."

Elwood appeared taken aback somewhat. "I guess I could. But that would mean my delaying the building of the tool shed."

"Of course," said Mr. Welton, "you just tell us what supplies you need, and I'll see you get them free of charge."

"For the tool shed?" Elwood asked.

"No, the bird bath."

Laughter ensued.

Then Elwood turned to address Billy Bob. "Billy, I understand your parents have been sending you to church day camp. Do you like it?"

Billy Bob looked at Elwood shyly, "Yes."

"Are you learning a lot?"

"I guess."

It was then that Mr. Welton broke in, "What do you mean 'you guess?' You either are or you aren't. Now, tell the Reverend yes or no."

"Okay, Dad," and Billy looked at Elwood, "yes or no."

"Humph," Mr. Welton snorted, "kids!" Then he turned to his daughter Julie. "You've been mighty quiet. What's going on?"

"Yeah," Elwood said, "I noticed the same thing about you, Elmo. Usually it's all we can do to get you to be quiet. What gives?"

"Ummm," Julie said.

"Elmo?" Elwood said prodding his son.

"Well, uh ..." Elmo replied.

"C'mon, you two!" said Mr. Welton, "are we going to have to play the game of twenty questions to draw you two into the dinner conversation?"

"I'm pregnant," Julie blurted out. "Could I have some more black-eyed peas?"

Dead silence ensued. Only Mrs. Welton had the presence of mind to pass the black-eyed peas. Finally she found her tongue. "And who is the father?"

Elmo hesitated at first, then said, "Ummm, I guess I am."

Mrs. Welton sighed, "What were the two of you thinking when you did this?"

Julie's expression looked strained. "Ummm, I dunno."

At that point, rage overtook Mr. Welton who bolted to his feet and lunged himself at Elmo, shouting, "You bastard! What have you done to my daughter?"

Just then Elwood got up from his chair and placed a conciliatory hand on Mr. Welton's shoulder. "Now, let's calm down. The kids have problems. Let's try to approach the matter rationally."

"Rationally!" Ellen screamed, "How can you be

so calm at a time like this!?" Then she turned to Elmo and yelled at him, "Elmo, how could you do such a thing? We didn't raise you... and have you given any thought as to what this will do to your father, his ministry... and what have you done to this girl!?"

Mr. Welton then broke in with, "All I can say is, if this bastard got my daughter pregnant, then by God, he's gonna marry her!"

"I agree," Elwood concurred.

"Dad!" exclaimed Elmo.

"Son," he said facing Elmo, "it's the honorable thing to do, and my son is going to do the honorable thing."

Elmo looked over at Julie and said, "Well, I guess I could do worse."

Julie looked at Elmo and smiled, "What a sweet thing to say."

"Marriage?" Mrs. Welton screamed. "They're not even dry behind the ears!"

Then she turned to Julie, "And Julie, what about your education?"

"Yes, Elmo," Ellen said breaking in, "and what about yours?"

Elwood sat in his chair, gave a waving gesture and said, "Look, we're all upset right now. I propose we take a little time to cool off and meet at the church in a couple of days; then we can figure where to go from here. Maybe we can consult with the wedding coordinator or maybe see what other alternatives are open to us."

"Elwood," Ellen cried, "how can you be so calm? Don't you realize what's happening here?"

"I've had practice," Elwood replied. "Remember Lawanda?"

"You're probably right," said Mr. Welton. "We do need to calm down. Right now, I don't have much of an appetite."

"I'd say that goes for all of us," Ellen replied.

"Does this mean no dessert?" Billy Bob chimed in.

"Hush, young man!" Mrs. Welton said.

Billy Bob then turned to Julie and said, "Gee, Sis, you sure know how to spoil a good dinner."

Two days later, the two families met in the church study along with the Reverend Franklin Marvin, the associate pastor. Pastor Marvin was a man in his late seventies, but unwilling to retire despite his increasingly frequent lapses into senility, to which he was often oblivious. He had served in the ministry for more than fifty years, most of that time being spent as a full pastor. His hair was gray, and he still had a full head of it. His complexion still had its color, and could easily pass for a man in his fifties. His energy level was high, but his memory was failing him.

As everyone got themselves situated and Billy Bob went out to play in the church playground, Elwood was the first to speak. "Okay, I hope we've all had time to cool off since Friday. I've a feeling we're going to need to remain calm if we're going to get through this thing successfully. Because it's a matter in which I'm personally involved, I felt it only proper to call in my colleague, Frank Marvin, to facilitate this meeting."

Elwood then turned to Frank. "Frank, I think we're going to need all the help we can muster. Could you lead us in prayer before we begin?"

"Most assuredly," Frank replied, "Let us pray." All present bowed their heads and closed their eyes. "Most merciful Heavenly Father," Frank began, "it is at this time that we, as your weak and unworthy servants, come to you humbly seeking your counsel. Our spirits may willfully seek to do thy will, yet our flesh is so weak and betrays these efforts. "

"Boy, is that ever right," Mr. Welton said.

"Shut your damn mouth!" Mrs. Welton snapped. "We're in prayer!"

"Yes," Frank stammered, "now where was I? Oh yes! We humbly ask you to impart your wisdom to us this hour as we bring these children before you."

"Oh, man," cried Elmo, "now we're really in for a lickin'!"

"Hush, Elmo!" Ellen growled.

"Well, there went my train of thought again," said Frank, flustered by all the interruptions. "Well, You know what needs doing here better than I do, Lord. So I call upon You to be sovereign in this situation and ask this in the name of Jesus Christ, our Lord and Savior. Amen." Frank then looked up and opened his eyes. "Okay," Frank continued, "Elwood briefed me a bit on what the issue is, but I'd like to hear what each of you has to say before giving you my thoughts on the matter." He turned to Mr. and Mrs. Welton, "Bob and Ella, I've known the two of you for many years. Your contribution to this church has been invaluable. I hope we'll be able to reciprocate in kind during this session." He turned to face Julie and Elmo and said, "And you two, hopefully the future pillars of this church -- though I may be getting a little advanced in years, I'm not as unaware as you might think I am. These are the seventies and, as a certain poet once said, 'the times they are a changing.' So, permit me to make one comment?"

"Sure, Reverend," Julie replied.

"Yeah, go ahead," Elmo echoed.

Frank then pointed his finger at both of them in stern admonition, "Shame, shame on you."

At that point Ellen whispered to Elwood, "Dear, are you sure it was wise bringing him in on this? I mean, really..."

Just then, Frank barked at Ellen, "There'll be no whisperin' in here! You got something to say, you say it so we all can hear it!"

"Okay, Pastor Marvin," Ellen said. "These are our children, and we expect you to handle this situation a little more professionally than...."

"All right," said Frank, "but even I'm entitled to a little emotion. When you've lived as long as I have and seen as much as I've seen, and seen how much has gone to Hell in a hand basket, then having to deal with stuff like this…"

"All right already!" Bob exclaimed. "Our kids are no prizes! We know that! Now, can we please get on with the discussion?"

"Okay," Frank conceded. He turned to Julie. "Julie, I understand you are now in a family way?"

"Well," said Julie as she grimaced, "I don't know about that, but I'm late with my period, so I think I'm pregnant."

"Have you ever been late before?"

"Never!" Bob interrupted. "You can set your clock by her!"

"Daddy," Julie whispered, "you're embarrassing me."

Then Frank turned to Elmo, "And you, young man, I take it you're the father and want to do the honorable thing by marrying her?"

"Damn, er… uh… I mean, you bet your life he does!" Elwood interrupted.

"Well," said Frank, "I guess the only thing that remains is the planning of the wedding. Of course, I hope you both have plans as to what to do once the knot is tied."

"I guess I'll have to get a job and, uh, maybe finish my education going to night school," Elmo replied.

"And where do you plan on living?"

Elwood then spoke up, "I guess they'll have to alternate between the Welton household and ours until they can get on their feet."

"Sounds like a plan," said Frank. "Not a good one, but I can't think of a better one, given the circumstances. Clearance for the wedding, of course, will have to be brought before the pulpit steering committee. Any idea what kind of a wedding the two of you would like?"

"A small one!" Bob said. "We'd kind of like this to be kept low profile."

"Bob," Frank said, "you're a deacon at this church. Your daughter's marrying the pastor's son. They're both in their mid-teens. Anyone here capable of putting two and two together is going to deduce that the two of them didn't enter into marriage voluntarily. So, I think you can kiss good-bye all hopes of maintaining a low profile here.

Word of this is going to leak out all over the church, and, as we all know, what leaks out in the church leaks out into the community."

"In that case," Julie chimed in, "can I have bridesmaids, and can I invite my girlfriends and their families, and can I have a shower... you know, a combination bridal and baby shower?"

"Hey!" Elmo shouted as he stood up, "If she has a shower, I want a bachelor party!"

"Over my dead body!" Julie screamed. "I'll be damned if I'm gonna let my husband-to-be go to some party to watch a naked girl pop out of a cake!"

"Hey," Elmo retorted, "a man's entitled to a last fling! It's the American way! Next thing you're probably goin' to tell me is I can't get drunk with my friends the night before! Boy, you women! First you get pregnant, then you cut the guy's balls off!"

"All right, you two!" Frank hollered. "Enough! There'll be time enough for domestic disputes after you've tied the knot! Right now, it might behoove all of you to discuss among yourselves what type of wedding you'd like to plan."

Julie then turned to her father, "Daddy, can we have a reception after the wedding, please?"

"A reception?" Bob countered. "Julie, do you realize how much something like this is going to cost?"

"Bob," Ella interrupted, "she is our only

daughter. Don't you think we owe her a little…"

"Dear, what about my plans to expand my business?"

"Well, you may have to put those plans on hold for now."

"But …"

"No 'buts,' Bob. If these two are going to get married, we might as well do it right."

"Oh, all right."

Then Elwood spoke up, "Bob, I believe seeing that it involves both our kids, my wife and I ought to go halves on the expenses."

"I agree," said Ellen. "And I'm so glad you made the offer, Elwood."

"Well," said Elwood, "how often does our son get married?"

"Wait a minute!" Elmo said. "I need a best man! I want my friend Kenny Buttkus to be my best man!"

"Who the hell, I mean heck is Kenny Buttkus?" Elwood asked.

"He's a guy I go to school with."

"Okay. Your choice."

"Well," said Frank, "I believe we're at least at a starting point." Then he brought out a booklet called a wedding planner. "This booklet might be of some help in the planning of the wedding, and there is indeed quite a bit of planning to be done."

Reverend Marvin's words were found to be heavily prone to understatement. Both the Weltons and the Pigginses not only had to plan, they also had to consult with vendors over numerous details involved in setting up the wedding. They visited the wedding boutique to choose Julie's bridal gown, her headpiece, her shoes, the dresses of her bridesmaids, and even accessories such as undergarments, jewelry, and a garter. Invitations were sent out. Musicians were hired. A caterer was consulted, and the florist too, regarding appropriate flower arrangements. The wedding cake was ordered from the bakery, along with the cake topper. Special napkins were ordered, along with guest favors. Elmo and Julie said they preferred the rice bags, much to the vexation of their parents, who knew how hard that stuff was to clean up and how much the church custodial staff would gripe about it.

They also ordered serving knives and toasting glasses. Julie wanted a photographer to take pictures of the event. When her father began to show concern over the expenses, his wife would say, "Hush! This is our only daughter, and it's probably going to be the only wedding she'll ever have. We owe it to her to make it a happy and memorable occasion."

"I don't know how happy it's going to be," Bob retorted, "but I don't think I'll ever be able to forget it. Neither will my business."

Finally, just two days before the wedding, the dress rehearsal was set to take place. All the members of the wedding party were present. The organist was right on cue as he played "The Wedding March." Down the aisle Julie went with her father. While walking Julie detected the presence of an old friend and whispered to her father, "Daddy~ I'm flowing."

"Yes, dear, I know," he responded, "I'm crying, too."

"No, Dad," she said, whispering louder than before, "1 mean, I'm flowing! I'm not pregnant after all!"

Bob stopped in mid-stride. "What?" he yelled.

Julie jumped up and down and yelled ecstatically, so that the entire wedding party could hear her, "I'm not pregnant! I'm not pregnant!" Of course, she was oblivious to the mess it was making on her dress.

All her bridesmaid friends gathered around her, hugging her, sharing in that jubilant moment. Elmo stood at the far end of the aisle near the lectern, looking up at his father and asked, "Does this mean there isn't going to be a wedding?"

"I think there might be a strong possibility of that being the case," Elwood answered.

"Gee, an' I got this hangover for nothing?"

Reflecting back on the enormous expenditures

that went into the preparation of the nuptials, Elwood said, "1 think I could use a stiff drink right now myself."

The impact of the wedding that never was remained on the minds of everyone even remotely touched by it. The parents of the community resolved to keep a closer watch on their adolescent progeny. They enforced more stringent curfew measures. They insisted their daughters dress more modestly. And many of the parents were adamant about their children giving a detailed account of their comings and goings.

As for Elmo and Julie, they were forbidden to see each other, unless a chaperone was present. That was fine with Elmo. The experience had left him shaken considerably. Elwood advised him to seek temperance from his youthful lust through means of prayer, meditation, and fasting. Of course, Elmo found another form of release to be more effective.

17

Elmo's education continued without any further threat of disruption. In high school, he got his fair share B's and C's, although he did excel in basketball and tennis, his gangly frame contributing to his skill. In football, he only attained a modicum of success, but he never let that deter him from trying out for the team. In his senior year, he made the varsity team. Yet, being only 150 pounds, he was relegated exclusively to a guard position. The duty of this position, the coach constantly informed him, was to, at all times, guard the quarterback, a 250-pound hulk named Bubba Wiggins.

During the last game of the season, college sports talent scouts were scattered about the high school stadium, and every member of the team was prepared to strut his stuff.

Just before the game, the coach, a burly man in his late thirties, came into the locker room to address the team. "Men," he shouted, "this is our last game. We win this one and we win first place in the division. Now, I know the college talent scouts are here, and I know that a lot of you are thinking about the fact that now's your chance to win that athletic scholarship. Well, that's fine. But I also want to remind you that we're still a team! That means that there are times when team obligations overtake one's individual wants and needs! That particularly holds true for all you guards! Yours might be a thankless task! But it's also an essential task! And that task is, at all times, to guard your quarterback! I cannot emphasize that strongly enough! We're here to play as a team, and we're here to win as a team! Now let's go out there and wipe the field with those bastards!"

The team shouted "Ho!" then departed the locker room psyched up for the game.

Elmo held tight to these words. The score was tied with only a few seconds left in the fourth quarter. A hulking quarterback by the name of Bubba Wiggins received the ball at the line of scrimmage.

Then, as Elmo ran along side of Bubba, an equally hulking member of the opposing team sought to tackle Bubba from the opposite end of the field. Bubba dodged just as another rushed toward him at a different angle. In a desperate lunge, Elmo leaped in front of the opposing team member, providing Bubba with the needed interference. The opposing team member landed on top of Elmo, knocking the wind out of him, bruising his ribcage, and inflicting him with a groin injury.

Bubba carried the ball all the way to a touchdown. Once over the goal line, Bubba threw down the ball and started jogging in place, yelling ecstatically as the crowd cheered. Bubba had won the game, the glory, and a football scholarship from the University of Alabama. As for Elmo, his only prize was a trip to the hospital.

Although a handful of friends and his immediate family gave recognition to his efforts, his contribution to the victory went largely unnoticed.

18

Graduation found Elmo in a directionless void. Not knowing which way to go in life, and bereft of any desire to seek spiritual insight on the matter, Elmo enlisted in the Navy. The night before Elmo was to ship out for basic training, his father sat him down to have a talk.

"Elmo," Elwood began as he looked over at his son from his desk in the church study, "I know over the years that you and I have had more than our fair share of disagreements. And I also know you felt any number of times that your mother and I unjustly imposed our will on you, forcing you to attend church and Sunday school every week, pressuring you to get baptized, spanking you when you were disobedient, insisting you do the honorable thing where Julie was concerned... but I want you to know this. Over the years, nothing has been higher on your mother's and my list of priorities than seeing that you and your sister were given the proper upbringing."

"I know that, Dad," Elmo said.

Elwood continued in a stern voice, "There are a few things I'm about to tell you that you may not know. One is, I freely admit that we failed with your sister, or she failed us. Right now, I'm really not too sure, and maybe I'm just too afraid to examine the matter as closely as I should. You, on the other hand, remain an open book. You're going into the Navy, and you're going to find it to be, at times, a rough and lonely place. I ought to know. During my hitch in the Navy I found there were times that the only things I had to fall back on and to keep me on an even keel were the love of God, my folks, and the values they tried to instill in me. It worked. I hope the same for you. In fact, you may find, as I found out, that the cohesive bond your family tried to instill in you might be the only thing you have to fall back on."

He then handed Elmo a Bible. "I want you to have this, too. The Lord and his teachings have been a very large part of your upbringing, and He still has a lot to teach you, if you'll let him. I think you'll discover that, when you're out on some prolonged sea duty."

19

Elmo found his father's words to be prophetic. It was during November of that same year that Elmo reported for basic training at The Great Lakes Naval Training Center in Great Lakes, Illinois. Having spent his life in South Carolina, Elmo was completely unprepared for the harsh meteorological contrast upon his arrival at the training center.

Winter was fast approaching, and already the weather was far below the point of freezing. The icy chill of the wind blowing in from Canada punctuated the inclement conditions.

The first thing to enter Elmo's mind after stepping off the bus with the rest of the recruits was getting warm. But such a luxury was not to be accorded him. Instead, Elmo and the rest of the recruits were summoned into formation out in the open air. They were then addressed by the recruit division commander, Chief Petty Officer Bertrand Fletcher. CPO Fletcher displayed all the attributes of a lifer. Although not quite forty, the wear and tear of military life had left their indelible markings on him. His face wore the visage of a hardened cynic. Every movement he made reflected the sentiment, "I don't give a damn."

Apparently oblivious to the cold, he appeared to harbor a sadistic delight in making his new charges endure the icy conditions as he droned on and on about what lay ahead during the course of the training they were about to embark upon.

The recruits were made to stand in line outside as they were issued their supplies, then there was the issuance of uniforms. During the issuance a man who called himself a tailor was present. He was a stocky man with a full-faced beard. He lined up the recruits according to height, then tossed the uniforms at them. The recruits were then informed quite emphatically by CPO Fletcher that during their copious 'free time' they would be responsible for most of the alterations. And he concluded with, "And if mommy and daddy didn't take the time to teach you girls how to sew, you'd better be a quick study, or God help you!"

Finally, just as Elmo was about to grow numb, he and his fellow recruits were taken to a wooden barracks that was not much warmer than the outside; this would be their quarters for the duration of their training.

Upon arrival CPO Fletcher told them to grab a bunk. Elmo noted there were no lockers in the barracks. Instead, CPO Fletcher instructed the recruits to place all their supplies into their sea bags.

After they had done so, they were commanded to hang their sea bags between the two horizontal stanchions adjacent to their bunks. They were then informed that the sea bags were to remain open and that they would be subject to inspection at any time.

Although Elmo was not truly cognizant of what was transpiring, it was clear he was feeling his first pangs of culture shock. Up to now, his horizons never extended too far beyond the parameters of Georgetown County. Because of his narrow frame of reference, he never dreamed there were so many different types of people, outlooks, and attitudes.

Among his fellow recruits were two Mexicans who came across the border seeking citizenship in the U.S. and, of course, a better life. Elmo had never seen a Mexican before. Being very limited in their ability to speak English and not knowing enough to pass the test for citizenship, they chose the high road: they opted to join the military. One of the Hispanic refugees informed CPO Fletcher that he did not "speak English good."

CPO Fletcher was totally bereft of all sympathy and told him, "Then you'd better listen real good during your training, 'cause I ain't doin' no spoon feedin'."

There were two California surfer types from San Diego; they suffered the most during the rigors of training. Having individualistic inclinations, hedonistic desires, and absolutely no feel for military bearing and protocol, they were continually running afoul with CPO Fletcher, mouthing off, being insubordinate, and not being able to keep pace with the rest of the squad.

On the opposite end of the spectrum was an Iowa farm boy named Lee Whittier. He reminded Elmo a lot of Bubba Wiggins. He was a rugged, handsome, and virile youth who was inclined to exemplify everything that was good in America. He excelled at everything, from calisthenics to close-order drill to anything else the training dished out.

It had been said that those from Iowa were known to make the best servicemen, and Lee seemed to bear out that supposed truism. In every undertaking, Lee was the epitome of physical fitness, mental acuteness, and superior attitude and adaptability.

But the most colorful of the recruits, to Elmo's mind, was a former New York taxi driver by the name of Hennessey. At twenty-seven, he already appeared outwardly as mean as his recruit division commander, yet more sinister in external show. He may not have been the strongest of all the recruits, but there could be no doubt he was definitely the meanest and the most ruthless. Everyone knew it was best not to mess with Hennessey. Even though many might be able to best him in a physical joust during waking hours, he was sure to get them back while they were sleeping. One time, he locked horns with Lee. Hennessey was doing his best to prod Lee into an altercation and was ultimately successful. Lee thoroughly bested him. It was then that Hennessey, while laying on the ground bruised and bleeding from the skirmish, looked up at Lee and snarled, "You gotta sleep sometime, mother fucker! And you'd better sleep with one eye open from now on!" Lee was sent to the infirmary a week later. Everybody knew who did him in, but nobody could prove anything.

During basic training Elmo endured rigors that made high school football practice appear easy by comparison. The recruits were required to do push-ups and sit-ups in the snow, and run for three-mile intervals with the wind piercing them through to the very core. They also were made to receive enough shots to make each one of them feel like human pincushions. After the shots, they did more exercises to take away the stiffness caused by the reaction.

The recruits also underwent numerous classroom sessions, with topics ranging from technical aspects of naval training to how to wear the uniform. On-the-job training was mandated in firefighting and the many other aspects relating to sea duty.

One morning, as snow flurries fiercely

hammered the landscape, CPO Fletcher gathered everyone in the squad together and announced that they were about to go swimming.

"In this weather?" Elmo shouted.

Fletcher got in Elmo's face, "'You got a problem with that, Sailor?"

Elmo found it in him to say, "No, sir."

CPO Fletcher then went on to say, "A war doesn't care what the weather's like. Therefore, neither does this training. Knowing what to do in the water under conditions such as these may save your life. And that's what I'm doing right now -- saving your lives."

"Yeah, if the hypothermia doesn't kill us in the process," one of the California recruits muttered.

"I didn't quite catch that. Sailor," CPO Fletcher barked.

"Nothing, sir."

"Good. Now, let's head for the pool."

The pool was in an enclosed outdoor area. The men were made to stand in a section elevated one hundred feet above the water, and there they were instructed to jump off the platform into the water. While immersed in the water they were instructed to remove their pants, tie a knot in the legs at both ends, then swing the pants overhead so they would catch air, enabling the pants to float. If the procedure was done properly, a float was structured via the pants.

Each man was required to undergo this exercise. If he was not successful, he was made to do it again and again until he was. Elmo got it right the second time and became totally numb during the process. Both the Mexicans got it right the first time. The California boys were the least successful; it took them five times to get it right, and they looked like they were going to die in the process.

Service week came two-thirds of the way into the training. During this time, the men were made to unload trucks for the galley and pull mess-hall duty. This meant increased exposure to the cold weather along with only three hours of sleep a night during the course of the week.

Basic training ultimately drew to an end. The next step, advanced training, tested Elmo mentally and emotionally, requiring him to either pass the rigors of the program or perish.

At last, Elmo was assigned his first sea duty. Exhaustion, by now, was Elmo's frequent companion. He was assigned a duty station while onboard. There, while in a grossly depleted state, he was barely able to complete the duties assigned to him. Yet, even in this state of acute fatigue, sleep was a very elusive commodity for young Elmo.

Nighttime would find him walking the deck or standing at the bow looking out at the sea. With nothing but water for as far as his vision would take him, the pangs of depression set in. It was then he remembered his father's words about the feelings of loneliness and isolation born out of conditions where a sense of community among even his peers was, too frequently, a nebulous commodity.

It was there, at sea, during the night, that Elmo experienced his first sense of brokenness, and, for the first time in what might have been ages, he began to pray, and pray intensely. From that prayer, he drew comfort, a sense of release, and, for perhaps the first time in his life, perceived feelings of divine guidance. It was then that Elmo gained his first sense of single-mindedness not unlike what the Apostle Paul, his first-century counterpart, sensed during his journey to Damascus. The desire to preach the Gospel and to tend to the things of God began to burn fiercely within his bosom. This sensation left him hungry for more, and he began praying with an even greater degree of passion and fervency.

As the days passed and as he continued pacing the deck of the ship, Elmo began reading the Bible his father had given him -- pouring over the text, committing verses to memory -- and his spirits began to soar. Many a night would find him walking the deck, praying, singing hymns, even uttering glossolalia -- speaking in the unknown tongues that

seemed to emanate from outside himself -- all the
while smiling effervescently, and laughing
exuberantly. It was an exhilarating feeling that
provided him with a great release. It renewed his
energy and revitalized his sense of purpose.

Word was soon brought to the captain of the
vessel regarding Elmo's behavior. Given the nature
of Elmo's bizarre conduct, the captain ordered him
to be tested for drugs. Elmo ran through a hasty
battery of tests, checking his heart and other vital
signs, and examining his eyes to see if he had any
head injuries. Finding nothing out of the ordinary,
the ship's physician transferred him to the quarters
of the ship's psychiatrist. The psychiatrist couldn't
find anything either, except Elmo's profession that
he was "high on Jesus!"

Given Elmo's ecstatic yet unassailable
response, the ship's psychiatrist was left with little
recourse but to release Elmo back to duty. At the
same time, the psychiatrist recommended that Elmo
be placed under strict observation and that his
activities be monitored as closely as possible. The
captain implemented this recommendation and
issued the appropriate orders to the ship's officers.
Elmo's constant smile and bubbly disposition was a
steady source of vexation to the officers, but they
found Elmo's work to be superior in quality. What
could they say? There was no law that said a sailor

onboard ship couldn't be a happy sailor, and Elmo's exuberant demeanor, bouncy gait, and positive spirit were having a contagious effect on the ship's morale.

Elmo would complete all the necessary tasks of his own duty station, then energetically rush about to other stations of duty, assisting his fellow sailors where he could, offering comfort, support, and consolation where it was needed, rendering encouragement where it was lacking, and bolstering the ship's overall esprit de corps. The enlisted men were putting more effort and enthusiasm into their work, cynicism and idle horseplay were cut to a minimum, and the ship on the whole was operating at peak efficiency.

In fact, based on the feedback the captain received, it appeared to him that he not only had the most efficient ship sailing the ocean, but also the happiest. He could live with the efficiency aspect of the ship, but the happy was a different matter. Somehow calling the crew into formation and being met with row upon row of sailors sporting ear-to-ear grins was something he was not prepared to address, even with all his years of experience as a naval commander.

One encounter found Elmo assisting a sailor at his duty station and offering him comfort in the process. The lad, no older than nineteen, just barely shaving because of his light blond hair, had received a 'Dear John' letter from his bride-to-be. The seaman was torn apart with sorrow, but Elmo brought up an unexpected contrasting overview to the seaman's plight. "That's good!" Elmo responded.

"Good!?" the seaman exclaimed.

"Sure," Elmo said. "That means the Lord has someone better in mind for you! That is, if you're in Christ!"

"Well," the seaman replied, "my folks never were much into religion and all, and I ... "

"Then we've got to get you saved right now so God can begin his miraculous work in your life!" Elmo said. "Let's kneel and have a word of prayer." And Elmo began, "Lord, we bring to You now a new sheep into the fold. He seeks Your will in his life now, Lord, as he comes to You." Then he turned to the seaman. "Do you accept the Lord Jesus Christ as your personal Lord and Savior?"

"Yes."

"Do you repent of all your sins and open your heart now to your new life in Jesus Christ?"

"Yes."

"Hallelujah! All Heaven is now rejoicing! And God has now prepared a place for you in Heaven!"

"But what about here? I don't expect to be going there for quite awhile."

"The Lord also has just the girl picked out for you, and she will be exactly the woman you need! Praise Jesus! Thank you, Lord!"

The ship's chaplain, on the other hand, was greatly bothered by this new trend. He was a Unitarian, and in spite of all his seminary and military chaplaincy training, he found he was lacking in the resources necessary to handle this spiritual awakening. The trend terrified him, and, much to his embarrassment, he found himself greatly angered by it. Elmo Piggins had gained himself so great a following onboard ship that the chaplain felt his office almost totally usurped, as he put it, "by some young upstart enlisted man." Only the officers attended his Sunday morning chapel services; the remainder of the crew congregated on the deck to hear Elmo preach.

One of the officers, a fresh-faced ensign just six months out of the naval academy, was walking the deck on a routine inspection, and went by the duty stations of various crewmen. During the course of this inspection, he asked a number of crewmen why they no longer attended the Sunday morning chapel services. All of them were quite adamant in their extolling of the charismatic dynamism of Elmo Piggins. "He is one man who truly knows Jesus!" One of the crewmen stated.

"But the ship's chaplain knows about Jesus

too," the officer countered.

"That's where the difference lies!" The crewman responded. "The ship's chaplain knows *about* Jesus! Elmo Piggins *knows* Jesus."

Hearing of this response, the ship's chaplain fell prey to a bout of depression. He ultimately resigned his post as chaplain and began looking into another career field.

20

Elmo excelled in everything the Navy tossed his way, and the time whizzed by for him. Near the end of his hitch, he had attained the rank of E5, second-class petty officer. For his exemplary service, those whose command he was under urged him to reenlist. He hadn't given it a thought. It was then he remembered the time just before entering the Navy, when he felt no inclination to ask for spiritual assistance regarding his life's journey. Since his stint in the Navy, so much had happened that he really did not have time to give any thought to the matter, but now, he figured, was the time to seek out the Lord's counsel on the issue.

In the solitude of his office, he went to his Heavenly Father for divine guidance. God's voice reverberated in Elmo's brain. This time the voice Elmo perceived was soft, yet firm and authoritative, leaving no room for ambiguity and giving clear and present sanctification to what his mission in life was to be. "You have been called into My service to preach the Gospel. Return home and tell your father that I have ordained it so."

"Well," Elmo responded, "who am I to argue

with God?" A few weeks later, his enlistment in the Navy was up. He notified his father and boarded a train back to Georgetown County. It would be good to see his family again.

During his naval hitch, he had been so absorbed with his ever-increasing military duties and so on fire with his newly acquired ministry that he was never able to see his way clear to visit his folks. He did write to them sporadically, but Elmo never was much good at communicating via the written word so the letters he did send his folks were terse and cryptic at best. His arrival home was destined to be fraught with many surprises for his parents, and perhaps for the church where his father was still the pastor.

His father and mother, along with a couple of the church elders, were there to meet him at the train station. His mother was the first to greet him with a tear-filled embrace. His father shook his son's hand and placed the other hand on his shoulder. "Man!" he exclaimed. "What did they feed you when you were in the Navy? You look like a rock!"

Elders Michael Jurgens and Joe Benson also joined in the greeting of Elmo. Elder Michael Jurgens, echoed his father's sentiments. "Your father's right! You have changed! I always say a hitch with Uncle Sam is what every boy needs to become a man."

"Amen!" said Joe Benson.

"Dad," said Elmo, grinning brightly, "I have something to tell you. And as long as you brought along a few of the elders, I figure now is as good a time as any."

"Sure, son. But can't it wait? We already arranged for your homecoming and ..."

"No. I don't think this can wait."

"Elmo," his mother interjected with a slight petulance in her voice, "what can be so all fired important that…"

"Mom," interrupted Elmo, "Dad, and the rest of you: I have received the call to preach the Gospel."

"Whaaaaat!" everybody exclaimed in unison.

"It's true!" exclaimed Elmo. "God has called me, and I feel determined to follow the leading of the Holy Spirit! I speak in tongues and ..."

"Wait a minute, son!" his father said, interrupting Elmo's proclamation. "Speaking in tongues? Your mother and I always tried to give you a good Christian upbringing, but this goes totally outside the realm of our influence. I have never endorsed such a practice. Do you truly know what tongue it is you're speaking in and where it's coming from? One of the things I tried so hard to teach both you and your sister is discernment, and based upon what you're telling me now, I don't believe I was very successful with either one of you.

And besides, you know as well as I do that anyone in this town who knows you and has watched you grow up, who's kept tabs on your past escapades, just will not lend any credence to your sudden conversion."

"Oh, well," Elmo shrugged, "some folks are just so full of the Devil, and besides, all I did to bring this about was follow the advice you gave me the day before I was shipped out for boot camp."

"Elmo," Joe Benson interjected, "if you're really on the level about this, I see no reason why we can't announce this at our service this next Sunday... even have a laying on of hands."

Michael concurred.

"How do you plan to pay for the schooling you'll need to follow in this endeavor?" Joe inquired.

"Well," replied Elmo, "I plan to work my way through, and my naval severance pay..."

"Will only take you so far," Michael interrupted. "1 suggest we introduce at our next church council session the issue of providing a scholarship for Elmo. What do y'all say?"

Joe voiced enthusiastic agreement.

"Well," Elwood replied, "this comes as a total surprise to me, but if you folks are all convinced of Elmo's calling, I guess the matter is settled. But you'll forgive me if I still have some reservations about the matter. I can't help but wonder what the Navy accomplished that I couldn't."

Elmo placed his hand on his father's shoulder, "Dad," Elmo replied, "it wasn't the Navy. It was Jesus!"

"Right," his father responded.

That evening, at home over supper, Elmo brought up another issue. "Mom! Dad! I've been praying about this, and the Lord has told me that my sister should be present in the congregation during this Sunday's service, when we have the laying on of hands."

His mother froze, and began to choke on her grits.

"Elmo," his father responded, "you know as well as your mother and I the situation with Lawanda. She hasn't been back to see us since the record burning. She walked out and swore she'd never set foot in the church again. So just what makes you think…"

"Daddy, the Lord has spoken to me and ..."

"Now, Elmo! I don't appreciate you pulling rank on me like that! You say you want to go into the ministry…"

"It's not what I want, Daddy. It's what the Lord wants."

"Okay, fine! But there are a few things you should know about the ministry. First off, there's more to ministry than just tossing out a bunch of God talk! Second, people have what's known as free will, and if Lawanda chooses the path she's on, then it's not up to us to dictate otherwise."

"But Daddy, the Lord wishes her to be in this service and He wishes for you, as her sire, to tell her so. This He has made clear to me."

"Okay. Then why hasn't He told me the same?"

"He has, Daddy. He's speaking through me."

Jumping up from his chair, Elwood leaned forward, pointing his finger at Elmo. "That is the most arrogant pronouncement I have ever heard come out of your mouth! To think that you could have the unabashed temerity ..."

"Now, dear," Elmo's mother interjected, placing her hand firmly upon Elwood's shoulder, "let's not lose our tempers. We owe it to ourselves to remain calm and rational about Lawanda."

Elwood sat back down in his chair. "All right. I'll be rational. I mean, what do I know? I've only been a minister for the past twenty-nine years. I've only spent seven years of college preparing myself to enter the profession, devoted myself constantly to continued education, seminars, updated training, research until I almost went crazy trying to get my doctorate... and then, my son, with no more than a high school diploma and a five-year hitch in the Navy under his belt, claims to know more of what the Lord wants than me. Who am I to dispute something as rational as that?"

"So, you'll call Lawanda?" Elmo asked.

Elwood froze, but quickly recovered. "Sure. I don't know what her number is. She hasn't written to us since her departure. All I know is that she lives in the Nashville area and she's enjoying a successful career in music. I'm sure she'd be more than willing to take time away from her musical bookings and recording engagements to travel all the way back to Georgetown County to watch her brother get hands laid upon him. So where do I begin? Nothing like reopening a family heartbreak ..." Elwood then got up from the table and headed for the phone. "I'll have to dial Nashville for information. I'm sure her number is listed. Lawanda Paget it is now, French sounding name -- trying to pass herself off as Cajun. Wouldn't even keep her family name." Heart pounding, Elwood picked up the phone.

21

"Dad! Dad!" Elwood could feel Elmo shaking him by his shoulders. "Are you all right?"

Elwood glanced tearfully at his son and put down the phone receiver. "I can't, Elmo."

"But Dad," Elmo persisted, "the Lord has spoken ..."

Elwood rose both in sorrow and in anger. "Didn't you hear me, Elmo? I said I can't!" He then rushed to the den.

Elmo headed after his father. "Elmo," Ellen said, "now is not the time!"

"But Mom, the Lord has spoken, and ..."

"Elmo, I know you believe what you say about the Lord, but..."

"Not what I believe, Mom! What His will be done!"

"Elmo," Ellen said, "this is very hard for your father, and your approach is all wrong! This is one thing you need to learn if you are going to go into the ministry -- timing! You also need to learn sensitivity, compassion, empathy, and sound judgment! Now I'll go talk to your father! You stay here and... talk to the Lord."

Ellen softly opened the den door. In the lamplight she could see her husband sitting on the couch, holding a picture of their daughter. "Elwood, dear..."

Elwood's voice was taut. "So many years. I wish it were that simple. I wish 1 could pick up the phone and talk to her. But God help me, I can't. I just can't."

Tears filled Ellen's eyes as she embraced her husband.

22

An hour passed. Elwood and Ellen emerged dry-eyed from the den and headed toward the phone. "Now, I want everybody to keep quiet!" Elwood demanded. "I don't know how I'm going to do this, but this is my responsibility, and I don't want you two to interfere."

"Excuse me?" Ellen protested. "She's my daughter, too!"

"All right," Elwood replied. "You can interfere." He turned to Elmo. "Elmo, I want you to keep quiet!"

"The Lord does move in mysterious ways," said Elmo. Looking upward he said, "Thank you Jesus. 0 li och bach li ach ku. Praise you, Lord Jesus."

"Elmo," Elwood retorted, "I said I wanted quiet! And I wasn't talking just to hear myself."

Minutes passed as Elwood dialed information, and dialed the various numbers given him. The idea of a celebrity having a listed number seemed highly unlikely, to Elwood's way of thinking. However, the information operator was quick to give a number for a Lawanda Paget in the Nashville area. Elwood felt a sharp twinge in his gut as he began to dial the number. What would his daughter have to say to him after so many years? What words could he find for her? He finished dialing the last digit and heard the phone ring on the other end. A woman's voice answered.

"Hello?"

"Lawanda Paget?" Elwood answered.

"Speaking." The voice sounded coarse and husky.

"This is your father, Lawanda," Elwood said.

"No way," the woman answered. "My father's been dead for the past seven years."

"Look, Lawanda," Elwood cried, "I can understand I may rate that, but at least..."

"No, mister," the voice responded, "I don't think you quite understand. I'm Lawanda Paget, the owner of the old Ko Ko Mo Truck and Rest Stop just off Nashville's outskirts. I'm sixty-five years old. My dad died seven years ago at the ripe old age of ninety-two. If he hadn't insisted on continuing to puff on them cigarettes and drink that straight whiskey, the old coot might still be alive today."

A calmness came over Elwood.

"Now, that other Lawanda Paget," the lady continued, "the country and western singer? That ain't even her real name. Her real name, if you can believe this, is Lawanda Piggins. Her first name's the same as mine, but I sure wouldn't want to go on stage with that last name."

"I can believe it!" cried Elwood. "I'm her father, Elwood Piggins."

"Well," the lady replied, "at least I know you ain't one of her crackpot fans tryin' to get through. She mentioned you occasionally, of course never to me directly. Sounded to me like you were guilty of tryin' to be a parent."

"Guilty as charged," Elwood sighed.

"Same here. These young 'uns today. I tell ya, you wanna beat them within an inch of their lives. Anyway, your daughter arrived at my truck stop a few years back – fought off a pimp at the bus station. A friend of hers she had been correspondin' with over the past few years worked at this stop."

Elwood sat there glued to the woman's every word. "This friend," Lawanda resumed, "introduced me to her. Well, I kinda felt sorry for the poor girl and let my sympathy get the best of my better judgment and I hired her on as a waitress -- let her sleep in a vacant bunk I had out in back. She wasn't the best waitress I ever hired, but she was a hard worker, your daughter. Sometimes she'd pull a double shift -- said she was tryin' to save up enough money to record a demo to send to Chet Atkins. I gotta say, she had one terrific voice. Use to hear her playin' her guitar and singin' out back after hours.

Well, we got this band that plays here three nights a week. One night, their female lead singer took ill with one terrific case of laryngitis and the band didn't know what they were gonna do. Then, Lawanda stepped up and volunteered to be her replacement. I swear, it was the first time I ever seen the crowd let out with a standin' ovation. I mean, usually the band was just noise, but this time, the crowd kept quiet for the most part and listened. I don't know what happened to the other lady singer, but one night there was this talent agent who heard the music and offered her and the band a contract. From then on, things just seemed to snowball. They didn't think Lawanda Piggins was a good stage name, so the agent asked to use my name for a certain share of your daughter's earnings--said it had a certain Cajun ring to it. I said why not. So, I been getting a varying passive income each month ever since. Been able to make some renovations to the truck stop with that extra money, and the publicity I receive from the deal ain't bad, either."

"I really appreciate you telling me this," Elwood replied. "Lawanda and I did not part on the best of terms and I just wanted to ..."

"Say no more," the lady interrupted. "It's time one of you started mending fences. Let me give you her number." The lady gave Elwood the number and wished him, "Godspeed and good luck."

Elwood took the number, thanked the lady, then hung up the phone and sighed.

23

After Elwood had finished sharing the news about Lawanda, Elmo spoke up. "That's all very interesting, Daddy, but we mustn't keep the Lord waiting."

"Elmo," Ellen snapped, "you are getting very annoying. Let your father and I be alone for awhile."

Elmo heeded and left.

After Elmo had left, she let out with a flustered growl of exasperation, "I swear! I don't know what's gotten into that boy! 'The Lord this,' and 'the Lord that!' I tell you, Elmo is making me furious!"

"He's right, though," Elwood responded. "It's been too long since our daughter's been lost to us. Even if she doesn't show up at this Sunday's service, we have to find a way to get in contact with her, just to let her know we're still here for her and we're listening -- maybe even to let her know we're her biggest fans."

"I suppose," Ellen sighed, "but I sure don't like our son's attitude."

"We'll worry about him later. Right now, come sit beside me. I need you to help me through this."

Ellen sat down beside Elwood, lending him a

supportive embrace. Elwood then proceeded to dial, and he and Ellen sat with their heads pressed against the receiver to hear what happened next on the other end of the line. The phone rang on the other end, and a feminine voice was heard.

"Hello."

"Lawanda Paget?" Elwood asked.

"Speaking."

"This is your father, Lawanda."

A click on the other end was heard. With trembling hands, Elwood dialed again. A voice answered on the other end.

"Please don't hang up on me, Lawanda," Elwood pleaded. "I'm calling to try to make amends."

"Amends? After all these years, you want to make amends?"

Elwood's voice was trembling. "I'd like to at least try, Lawanda. But I don't know exactly where to begin. I was sort of prodded into this by your brother, but it's also something both your mother and I want to do."

"What about my brother?"

"Well, he says he wants to be a minister ... well, he says the Lord wants him to preach the Gospel. He also says the Lord wants me to patch things up between us."

"Daddy, I really don't care to be preached to."

Elwood's voice cracked, "And I'm not going to preach to you, Lawanda. Maybe because ... well, maybe because I went about things all wrong with you. I don't know at this point. All I know is that I love you, I've missed you terribly all these years, and ... God, I don't know what else I can say to you! I confronted your supplier, because I couldn't bear the thought of him polluting you with that poison! I beat up your boyfriend, because I couldn't stand the thought of him defiling my baby! And maybe I was wrong to listen to Reverend Meachum. I don't know. I was the last pastor in Georgetown County to hold out on that record burning, and even to this day I don't know if I made the right decision to go along with it, but that necklace, and those awful back-masked messages! In the best way I knew how, I acted out of concern for your soul." Elwood's voice was fraught with anguish and desperation.

Ellen took the phone. "Lawanda, this is your mother. I've missed you, too. Your father and I both love you very much. Our lives have been so empty since you went away. I know we've made mistakes with you, but if you just give us another chance, I swear we'll try to be the best parents to you that we can." Ellen's voice was trembling and it cracked a few times during her discourse, like her husband's. "We're going to have a special service for your brother Elmo this Sunday -- a laying on of hands before he embarks upon his preparation for the ministry. He's also going to give the sermon. He wants you to be there. We want you there. We can use it as a time of healing. Please say yes, Lawanda. Please."

Lawanda replied, "Oh, you want me to drop everything I'm doing now with my life to attend his church service because he's following in his dear daddy's footsteps? I never heard of either of you coming to one of my concerts."

Elwood took the phone. "You're right, Lawanda, we didn't. But we've bought all your records several times, because we played them so much, we wore them out and had to buy new ones -- and we wore those out, too. And talk about scrapbooks -- I don't think any of your fans have followed your career as closely as your mother and me. We have volumes of articles about you, your love interests, your concerts. We check the TV Guide very closely to see if you're on any programs during the week, and we've recorded them all on the VCR! And played them over and over! It's the next best thing to having you here with us! I swear, Lawanda, it's true!"

"You bought my records?" asked Lawanda.

"Every one," Elwood replied.

"Did you check for any satanic back messages?"

"No, I didn't. We didn't. We don't care if you sing a duet with the Devil himself, as long as there's you on the record singing."

"You mean that, Daddy?"

"With all my heart, Lawanda. With all my heart. Please come home."

"Well... I don't know ..."

"Lawanda," Elwood spoke with firmness in his voice, "if you say no to me now I'm prepared to come to Nashville, hunt you down, and do something I'm really not too good at, but if I thought it would get you to come, I'd be willing to give it a try!"

"And what might that be?"

"You want to see me on my knees?"

Lawanda sighed, "All right, Daddy. I'll have to do some juggling of my schedule, but I'll do my best to make it home this Sunday."

"Thank you, Lawanda! Thank you so much!"

Elmo returned home and received the news from his folks. "Hallelujah!" he cried, "The Lord's will be done! But Daddy, you should have told her that the Lord desires her presence!"

"Elmo," Ellen snapped, "shut up!"

24

Lawanda arrived the day before the church service. Both she and her parents had much to catch up on. Lawanda was gracious enough to bring her parents copies of her not-yet-released recordings and assorted publicity paraphernalia. Elwood and Ellen received these gifts and held them tightly as if they were gold.

That Sunday, during church service, Reverend Elwood Piggins announced his son's intent while the elders called upon the congregation for a laying on of hands. Lengthy and extensive prayers were offered up on Elmo's behalf. Then, after the ritual of hands reached its conclusion, Elmo stepped up to the pulpit to deliver his first sermon.

Elmo began with a brief and quiet prayer. "0 Heavenly Father, let Your blessings shower down in great abundance this hour on Your house, and upon this time of worship. We ask this blessing in the holy name of Jesus -- Amen, Amen, and again I say Amen." Elmo then spoke boldly as he began his sermon. "It sure is wonderful to be in the house of God today! Do I hear an Amen?"

There was silence in the congregation.

"Do I hear an Amen?" Elmo shouted with even greater boldness and power.

A select group of parishioners tentatively shouted "Amen!"

Elmo continued, "With all the discord, violence, tumult, distress, and dysfunction out there in the world today, truly the house of God is the best place to be. Before we, as believers, abide for a time within this house, we take from this house the inspiration to be salt to a world so desperately void of and so greatly in need of the saltiness only we, as Christians, can offer. Do I hear an Amen?"

Learning their lesson from the last cue, more of the congregation boldly said, "Amen."

"Much is said in God's own word on the importance of having God within the realm of your household, because without His presence among us, this church, the church I so fondly remember my sister and I growing up in and receiving spiritual sustenance from, becomes just another building. There is a passage in Joshua, I believe, that says it best. If you would turn with me to Joshua, chapter 24, verse 15; and if you would read with me; 'Now if you are unwilling to serve the Lord, choose this day whom you will serve, whether the gods your ancestors served in the region beyond the river, or the gods of the Amorites, in whose land you are living; but as for me and my household, we will serve the Lord.' And on that note, do I hear an Amen?"

Again the congregation chimed in with "Amen."

"You'd better believe, Amen!" Elmo had picked this bit of rhetoric up from the Pentecostal minister Michael Davis.

Elmo resumed his talk as he moved from the lectern and down the steps, until he was standing amid the congregation. "I remember many a time when I would watch on TV the dropping of the ball in Times Square on New Year's Eve... signaling the start of a new year. I remember the excitement people would show as they sang jubilantly the age old tune commemorating the tossing off of the old and the bringing on of the new 'Auld Lang Syne!' I remember all the cheering, the hugging, the kissing-- truly it was a big event here on this dull, earthly sphere -- but you know, in the realm of the Heavenlies, it didn't even register! But oh, how glorious it is when just one sinner is saved ... when one lost sheep is found and brought back to the fold! So truly, I am in great anticipation this hour, because I know that, even now, as I speak to you, God is speaking to someone's heart maybe softly, 'you need Me, you need Me!' And that tiny, tiny voice is getting bolder and bolder as each moment passes." And his voice grew louder and louder. "Lord, I pray this hour that my voice can lend itself to help amplify the conviction being laid on that soul, that I might serve as a conduit for the Lord's purpose! 0 li 0 li acum su bach a lichum! I pray come quickly, Lord Jesus!"

The congregation grew somewhat frenzied at this point. They were not a gathering that was accustomed to glossolalia, nor were they used to having a speaker deliver a message with so much fervor and intensity. Many of the members became caught up in the charisma Elmo exuded. Others exhibited shock and uneasiness. But Elmo remained oblivious to his audience's reaction. He had a message to deliver—a message sent down by God Almighty—a message that needed to be heard, and Elmo was going to make sure it was heard, and by Elmo's reckoning, God's words were going to stick and stick hard.

Elmo continued to preach. "I remember as a boy, being the pastor's son, I was continually brought to an awareness of that voice. Yet it was Satan who fueled my own stubborn will and kept me from allowing the leading of the Holy Spirit in my life. It wasn't until after I joined the Navy and experienced being away from home for the first time, I felt that aching feeling of aloneness. I felt that profound feeling of brokenness … and that's what it takes, good brethren! It takes brokenness! It is at that time of brokenness when you are most open to God's leading and when God can truly use you! It is that sense of brokenness that I pray for you this hour! The time for it is now! There may be no tomorrow!"

Elmo's voice demonstrated a gradual heightening of passion. "I remember a story I once heard about shepherds and sheep. Jesus often called his followers His sheep. Now, why would He call them His sheep? Let me tell you, it was no compliment!"

The congregation let loose with uneasy laughter. "Sheep are dumb animals. They don't know where or how to forage for the right food. The shepherd has to lead them to food. There's a verse in the twenty-third Psalm about the shepherd leading his sheep beside the still water. Often times, the shepherd had to dig pools of still water for the sheep to drink from. Otherwise the sheep would fall into the currents of rushing rivers and drown. And there were times when the sheep would wander from the fold and get lost. When this happened, it became necessary for the shepherd to break the leg of the sheep. While the sheep's leg was healing the shepherd had to carry it, and the sheep became more and more dependent on the shepherd until a strong bond was built between the sheep and the shepherd. So strong was that bond that the sheep, even after its leg was healed, would never be inclined to wander again from the fold."

Elmo then shouted, "The Lord broke me, folks! I must now follow the leading of the Holy Spirit, because that's my lifeline! I know now, the independent spirit is a spirit that kills! I was dying without the Holy Spirit's leading! But like the sheep, I was too dumb to know! But the Lord showed me! He opened my eyes! He took me and He said, 'You're Mine, Elmo Piggins! You're Mine!'"

The congregation was now on the edge of their seats, taking in Elmo's every word, movement, and gesture.

"And there is someone else in this congregation, good brethren," Elmo continued, "someone else to whom the Lord is now reaching out! Someone who is known to us all, but has long been lost on that broad highway of sin and destruction... a sheep the Lord has been desperately seeking out to draw back into the fold! One in whom the fires of rebellion burned hot, but the Lord is now seeking to quench with His love and lead beside the still waters! On bended knees, I reach out my arms in love to this person and extend the words God has given me to say!" And Elmo walked over to the pew his sister was occupying and pointed his finger in her face, "Lawanda Piggins, I am not going to mince any words with you! You need Jesus! You need

Jesus! You need Him!"

Enraged by her brother's audacity and the spectacle he was making of her, Lawanda stood up, walked over to where Elmo was standing, and slugged him twice -- once in the face and once in the solar plexus. She then turned and yelled with fury, "This is what I came back for, Daddy? You can all go to Hell!" And she turned and ran out the door.

Elwood started after his daughter but was restrained by Ellen. "No, Elwood," she said. "You'd better stay here to clean up the mess Elmo just made. I'll go after her. I could just kill Elmo."

The congregation started to get out of their seats and move toward the exit when Elmo, with a commanding presence, motioned them back to their seats and continued his sermon. Like obedient children, they moved in clusters back to their seats.

"That hurt folks!" he said. "That hurt a lot!" Elmo felt his face and saw blood on his hands. Then he looked up and faced the congregation. "But as much as that hurt me, it comes nowhere close to the hurt God feels when He is rejected. You can see that she's smaller than me. She's not as strong as me. But when she's a mind to, she can put a powerful hurt on me. And that's how it is with God, my dear brethren. He's bigger than you. He's far more powerful than you. But by your words ... by your attitudes of rejection, you can put a powerful hurt on

Him! That's right! The King of the universe, but weak, insignificant you can hurt Him mightily with your words of rejection."

Elmo continued speaking with a fervency that rivaled a Billy Graham or an Oral Roberts. He held the parishioners spellbound by his charisma and conviction. At the conclusion of the sermon, Elmo made an altar call. Half of the congregation came forward to be saved, whether they needed to be or not. There was singing, rejoicing, and people speaking in tongues all around the church.

Most of the elders gathered around Elwood, shaking his hand and gifting him with plaudits. One of the elders, Barry Whitson, a sandy-haired man in his early thirties, said, "This is the greatest thing to happen to this church since the record burning!"

Michael Jurgens said to Elwood, "I think that son of yours could lead this church to a revival!"

"You should be very proud of your son!" said Joe Benson.

But not all feedback was positive. As the parishioners left the building, Reverend Elwood Piggins overheard, "Leading of the Holy Spirit, my ass!" Deacon Bob Welton snapped, "That's the same son of a bitch that damn near impregnated our daughter!"

"Hush, Bob," responded Mrs. Welton, "we're in church."

"In church? You think I give a damn? I swear, that travesty of a service is enough to make me want to swear off the whole damn religion!"

Simultaneously, Elwood half-heard another parishioner saying to her husband, "I guess it's true the Lord works in mysterious ways, but I never believed He had such a sick sense of humor."

"Now, Gladys," her husband replied, "it's not our place to criticize."

"No! Like mindless sheep, we just go along with the program."

Finally, Deacon Lee Hayes, an elderly man closing in on eighty, with a head full of gray hair and an equally graying face, spoke directly to Elwood. "You know, Reverend, there's a reason I come to this church and stay away from the Holy Roller Church."

"Believe me, sir," replied Elwood, "this is as big a surprise to me as it is to you." Elwood felt embarrassed and quite ill-at-ease after hearing these remarks. Meanwhile, Elmo basked in the glory of congregational plaudits, amens, and praises, all the while reminding those about him that he was only God's instrument and the real praise belonged to the Lord Himself. Elwood turned to Michael Jurgens. "Look, I know I'm supposed to be the official hand shaker, but it looks like Elmo has the congregation occupied, and there's a situation at home that I believe requires my attendance."

"No problem," said Michael. "We'll probably be by your place later on, though. This has been one terrific service. I have never seen things so lively and spirited. I truly believe we've been blessed today!"

Elwood was quick to dismiss himself. He was afraid of saying something he might regret later. He headed straight for home, and upon his arrival, Ellen met him in the driveway. "Where's Lawanda?" he asked with a desperate tremor in his voice.

"Gone," Ellen replied. "She was so angry. Whatever chance we had for a reconciliation..."

"No!" Elwood shouted. He slammed his fist into the hood of the car.

Anxious minutes passed while Ellen and Elwood discussed the morning's events, until they heard the honking of horns approaching from down the street. Soon a procession of cars carrying Elmo, the elders, and a host of elated parishioners reached the Piggins' house. Everyone gathered around Elmo, smiling, shaking his hand, patting him on the back and singing praises to God. "I've never felt so blessed by a service!" said Marlene Ponks, a chubby and robust woman in her mid-fifties.

Seth Wiggens, Sr., a balding, slightly framed man in his late fifties, exclaimed that he felt that the Lord had put a conviction upon his heart and on that of his wife's to volunteer for mission work in the Congo.

Joe Benson stepped up to Elwood and said, "This son of yours is truly sent by God. Anything he needs to complete his education, you can count on us and the church to deliver. It would be a sin for us to do any less."

Elmo had an ear-to-ear smile. "I feel so blessed, right now!" he said addressing the crowd. "Never has following the Lord's will felt so good! And I feel so grateful to all of you!" He then turned to Elwood smiling and asked, "Say! Where's Sis?"

"Gone," was Elwood's somber reply.

"Good!" Elmo replied. "The Lord has seen His work done here today! Now, wherever Lawanda goes, God goes with her!"

"You should be very proud of your son!" said Marlene Ponks almost in tears.

"Well," said Elmo, "I need to finish packing! The summer session starts in just two days and I want to be ready!" Within the span of two hours the crowd of people had gone home and Elmo had jubilantly driven off to college.

"You know, dear," Elwood said as the two of them stood in the driveway, "I'm giving serious thought to resigning from the ministry."

"Could you tell me why?" Ellen asked.

"Because of what I'm thinking right now."

25

It was summer, and another sweltering and humid day below the Mason Dixon line. Elmo Piggins drove his vehicle steadily northwards amid the pine, oak, palmetto, and green rolling hills that decorated the landscape along U.S. Highway 501, taking him away from his home in Georgetown County, South Carolina, to a destination that lay in the central most region of the American continent. His steely blue eyes fixed themselves intently on the road ahead. His facial features, replete with solidly squared cheeks and firmly jutted jaw, assumed a jubilant yet solemn and purposeful expression. He would soon connect up with Highway 76, heading westward to a flatter terrain on the Cherokee Strip and with an obscure town in the state of Oklahoma.

It was in this town that an equally obscure Christian liberal arts college and graduate theological seminary were situated. The college enrolled approximately two thousand students and was an integral part of many family traditions. Elmo's family played a vital role in the maintenance of that tradition. It was there that his father did his undergraduate work, attained his Masters of Divinity degree, and ultimately his Doctorate in Ministry. Elmo would continue to uphold that proud tradition; he would embark upon a six-year preparatory mission he knew he had been divinely commissioned to undertake. No doubt existed in his mind. It was to be his calling in life to preach the Gospel and tend to the things of God.

Elmo got on highway 76. He would arrive at his destination that evening and check into the men's dormitory at the university. He felt wonderful. His grades were only Bs and Cs in high school, but he felt confident that with the Lord by his side, he would get straight As.

The undergraduate program traditionally lasted four years; he was determined to get through in three years or less, then quickly begin his seminary studies.

Elmo smiled joyously as he proceeded down the road toward his destination. His heart was light and his spirits soared.

THE REBIRTH OF
REGINALD DEXTER

1

It was the end of the spring quarter at the University of Oklahoma in Norman. Dr. Reginald Dexter sat at his desk looking over the empty room that was his office for more years than he cared to imagine. He heaved a sigh, partially out of melancholy, but mostly out of disgust. "Sixty-five years old and they toss you out like so much garbage," he mumbled to himself.

Dr. Reginald Dexter, Ph.D., Psych. D. and soon-to-be Professor Emeritus of the Department of Psychology, having already posted his grades and now tending to the task of clearing out his office space, turned his mind to the unhappy prospect of retirement. It was not a retirement of his choosing. After turning sixty-five during the spring quarter, he had been alerted to the necessity of leaving by both the department heads and the university board of regents. Without much warning, Dr. Dexter was hailed and farewelled in the form of a commemorative banquet, as well as being accorded a gold watch for his thirty-five years of faithful service, along with the official notice of the terms of his pension plan. These two items, along with his

Social Security, would afford him a modestly comfortable lifestyle.

Still, the thought of retirement was something Dr. Dexter did not relish. In spite of his chronological age, Reginald remained a strong, stout, and hale figure of manliness, endowed with brown, wavy locks only slightly tinged with gray around the temples. His physique was trim, the result of a disciplined exercise program consisting of a combination of rigorous calisthenics, jogging, and swimming laps in the campus pool—activities that still attracted female student onlookers and aroused the ire of their male counterparts.

Of course, Dr. Dexter had renounced the rakish activities that consumed him in his earlier days and was now bound up in a matrimonial union with a woman with whom he shared a passionate and loving commitment. He was ecstatically happy in this monogamous relationship, except for the fact that, since he was over twenty years her senior, it was unlikely that she would be inclined to join him in retirement. She was presently ensconced as a partner in a thriving legal practice and would not hear any notions of surrendering her position in the firm, nor would he want her to. Dr. Dexter always contended that one of the keys to a happy and successful marriage was the affirmation of each partner with regards to the ambitions of the other, an affirmation that included aiding them in realizing their dreams. Reginald believed in this concept wholeheartedly. But now he stood alone, faced with his own sense of isolation and loss of purpose.

Carrying out the last of the file boxes, Reginald found himself remembering the words of a poem by Dylan Thomas: "Do not go gentle into that good night, Rage, rage against the coming light ..."

Suddenly overcome with foreboding, Reginald headed toward his car and drove to the Unitarian Church to see his longtime friend and pastor, Dr. Kenneth Green. Dr. Green, Reginald's peer both in cerebral prowess and chronology, although admittedly his superior in matters transcendent, was quick to latch onto the crux of Reginald's concerns. Once having heard, Reginald fell silent as Ken leaned back in his chair and proceeded to offer advice.

"If I were to ascribe to Jung's postulates," he said, "I would say you have much to negotiate, regarding your own death."

Reginald's face took on a look of shock at Ken's pronouncement as his facial features took on a loss of color

"I can see by your expression, my friend, that I've struck a nerve. But it's really all quite simple. Everyone leaves this plane of existence at one time or another. It's how we live while we're here that counts. I've had to go through this myself, you know."

"You have?" Reginald stared at him curiously. As far as he knew, this was a man who would probably never stop working.

Ken abruptly rose from his desk. "Oh, yes! I'm five years younger than you, but I figure you'll outlast me by several years. I drink, I smoke, and I consume more than my fair share of junk food for a man my age. I anticipate I have about ten more years. In another three, I intend to retire. I'm pretty certain I can gauge what needs to be done during the remaining years," he went on, "and I can state quite confidently that then I will be able to pass onto the next plane of existence with relative ease."

Reginald leaned forward, struggling to grasp the meaning of Ken's words. "So, let me see if I understand you correctly," he said. "You're telling me that in order for me to live successfully for my remaining years, I have to know how to die?"

"Precisely!" Ken replied. "But it goes deeper than that. You also have to find a way to see that you do not die before your death!" Ken folded his arms over his chest, and gave Reginald a knowing look. "Just add a couple of things to your lifestyle in general and you could break a hundred. If you don't figure out what to do with your life between now and then, well, your time left on this plane could be cut a bit more abruptly."

Reginald's heart thumped a little faster. "Okay," he said, "but how do you suggest I go about this?"

"Glad you asked, Reggie, old man!" Ken said, assuming a self-satisfied smile.

"And quit calling me 'old man!'" Reginald grumbled.

"Sorry. I just find that a little bit of levity tends to brighten what might at first appear like a grim undertaking ... and I guess I shouldn't use the word 'undertaking' either. But with that said, let me 'plot' out a proposed course for you."

"You're a real barrel of laughs today, aren't you?" Reginald said glumly.

"I've found, and you will, too," his friend told him, "that once you embark upon this process, you will find humor in things you never dreamed of. Trust me. It's a truly liberating experience. And it can be fun, too. First, I've known you for many years now, and I believe you have always had a penchant for intellectual endeavors. Matter of fact, I've read many of your works. Quite fascinating. So fascinating, in fact, that I would suspect that you are still thirsty for knowledge. Now, your field is psychology?"

"Right," Reginald said impatiently. He was really anxious for Ken to get to the point.

"Then you must know as well as I do that psychology was once described as the study of the human soul. After all, psyche and soul are synonyms. And I'm sure you're familiar with the fact that psychology is an integral part of the Buddhist and Taoist religions and has also dribbled over into the makeup of other religions, as well. The only problem is that it tends to confine itself to the here and now. But it has a cousin that picks up where it leaves off."

"And what might that 'cousin' be?"

"Theology, man!" Ken said, rocking back and forth from heels to toes. "I guarantee that if you immerse yourself in that study, I'm almost certain you will find the answers you seek. And that's not all. I have some other ideas that you'll find interesting."

"You might?" Reginald looked blank.

"Haven't I mentioned that I was planning on retiring from the ministry in another three years? That's how long the program in theological studies generally takes, if you keep your old nose to the proverbial grindstone. The people at this church know you, they respect you, and I don't think it would take very much convincing on my part to have them see that you would be the perfect man to replace me when the time comes. What do you say? You'd get one more set of initials after your name, another chance to satisfy your almost unquenchable thirst for knowledge, exposure to these transcendent issues that need contending with, and the opportunity to serve as pastor of this church for, say, the next fifty or sixty years?"

They both shared in a hearty laugh. Reginald was starting to warm up to the idea. The wheels were spinning. Then, leaning forward in his chair, he posed the question, "So, where do I go to study theology?"

"Well," Ken replied, "if this were Northern California, I'd recommend the place where I got my Masters of Divinity: Starr King Theological Seminary. However, there's no Unitarian seminary here in Oklahoma. So, you'd need to follow your course of study at a more Trinitarian seminary."

"And where might that be?"

"It's about one hundred and fifty miles north of here," Ken told him "I can get you the literature on it right now. It's a place called Parkins Theological Seminary. I have a catalog on the place in the church library. Follow me."

After skimming through the Parkin's Theological Seminary catalogue that Ken provided him with, Reginald expressed some guarded interest. "It might be a bit of a rush job trying to get in on such short notice, but I don't anticipate you'll have any problems," he explained. "That Dr. Archibald

Shyster, the current dean of the seminary, is always hungry for students. And just a side note, Reggie, beware of that guy. I've known him off and on for years, and he's one man who lives up to his name. He may claim to promote the Christian way of life, but he's one of the biggest con artists you'll ever find walking the face of this planet. I always thought religious convictions sensitized the human conscience, and in many people, they do. But then you run into a man like Dr. Shyster—I tell you, he has got to be the biggest horse's ass—but that'll be a learning experience for you too, Reggie."

"Like I haven't had to deal with horse's asses before," Reginald said dryly.

Ken set the catalog aside. "Now," he said, "summer's going to be twelve weeks, which leaves you the entire summer to occupy yourself in a range of new activities. It's no joke, Reggie! These summer months will be critical for you in working through this process."

Selecting an armful of books from the shelves, Ken piled them in Reginald's arms. "I'd like for you to familiarize yourself with this 'cousin' of your life's discipline," he said placing a companionable hand on Reginald's shoulder. "I believe you will draw some interesting parallels between the two. And along with theology, I've also selected a few books that deal with metaphysics. I want you to read and digest them all before the fall semester. And there's one more thing."

"As if this reading isn't enough?" Reginald responded, visions of long anticipated weekend excursions with his wife fading.

"No," Ken replied emphatically. "And this is even more critical than the reading. I want you to extend yourself in other ways, namely recreation. You've established a general exercise routine over the years. I want you to expand that routine by exploring the practice of tai chi."

"Tai chi?" Reginald responded.

"Yes, tai chi." Ken replied, launching into an on guard move, one knee bent and his own right arm extended. "These are stylized forms of warlike movements developed by the Chinese as exercises to tone you physically, mentally and spiritually, which is suppose to summon the 'chi,'—the discipline connected with the drawing up of energy. I believe you will find the techniques offered in tai chi quite useful. Next," he said, righting himself, "I'd like for you to do some things you've never done before, and probably would never dream of doing—some things that involve risk taking, maybe even an element of danger. Activities that will take you outside the realm of your established 'safety zone.'"

Reginald felt somewhat overwhelmed. "Like what?" he demanded.

The pastor hopped about with his arms in the air. "Skydiving!" he cried.

Reginald was overcome with shock at his friend's pronouncement. "Whaaaat?!" Reginald exclaimed.

"I've tried it!" he assured his friend who was giving every sign of backing from the room. "You will find it a most exhilarating experience! Food will taste better, the air you breathe will be sweeter, sex will be more satisfying ..."

"No way!" Reginald assured him. "That's crazy! At my age? Forget it! I could get killed!"

"And that's the entire point," Ken said. "I'm serious! Risk-taking should be a vital part of your life now! It will help to bring matters into perspective ... to make you aware of what's important to you and what isn't. Having your life flash before your eyes makes you really focus!"

Ken's suggestion left Reginald stunned. "Is this just another way of getting rid of us old codgers?" he demanded. "First you retire them, then you kill them off with craziness!"

"That may be one way of looking at things," Ken said. "But then, some of us may survive that craziness and come back as virtual leviathans, bursting with the ability to take whatever the world tosses our way and throw it right back! By the way, after you master skydiving, you might consider pursuing other recreational ventures."

Reginald sighed. "And what might these 'ventures' be?"

"Well," Ken said thoughtfully, "I'm thinking of dirt-bike riding, sports-car racing, windsurfing, horseback riding, hang gliding … then …" and he looked directly at Reginald, "if you can get around to it, there's a spot in Colorado I'd like for you to visit where another pastime is coming into popularity. Bungee jumping!"

At this point, Reginald began to feel irritated. "Hey look, this all seems really wild, but my wife …" he began.

"Eleanor?" Ken said. "What about her? Didn't you once tell me that she's up to her neck in legalese?"

"Well, yes, but …"

"And anybody that's seen you two together can guess that there's quite a difference in your ages. Reggie, you are presently reaping the bitter fruits from the wild seeds you sowed back in your heyday. I remember reading an article about the importance we grant those close to us at given periods in our lives. At sixty-five and over, the husbands and wives once again assume the position of number one in their respective mate's life. Up to that point, they were in last place. You may cast her as number one in your life right now, but I don't believe the reverse in true."

Reginald was offended. "How can you say that? You hardly know her! She loves me."

"Love has nothing to do with it," Ken told him smugly. "She loves you, I can tell. But you know that you're not her first priority. So, unless you think you can join her in her legal practice, maybe become her legal researcher or something like that, you'll just have to live with that reality. And if you don't believe what I'm saying is true, just step back and observe how she reacts to you tonight. It may be a bitter pill to swallow, but you have presently reached a point in your life where you'll have to prove that you're worthy of being kept around. You have to earn the right to be in life's mainstream instead of finding yourself the victim of the conventional theory that sees you as someone ready for the human scrap heap."

"Human scrap heap!?" Reginald cried. "What do you mean by that?"

"Exactly that," Ken babbled on. "I was watching this futuristic drama on PBS the other night. The production depicted a totally barbaric portrait of this future society where the men, after they had reached a certain age, were given a commemorative banquet, and afterwards, they were obligated to kill themselves. One of these men meets a woman from another culture, falls in love with her, and decides he wants to go on living. But his culture gets the better of him. Confronted by the shock and outrage of his family, he proceeds with the age old ritual and dies." Ken looked so outraged that, for a moment, Reginald wanted to laugh. But the man had made his point. "We're a good deal like that, you know," he went on. "Once you're retired, you might as well be thrown in the garbage. But you have a right to go on living, but you've got to take bold steps to claim that right! And now is the time to begin!"

2

That evening, in his stucco suburban home near the campus, Reginald busied himself fixing dinner for Eleanor, after which, noting her preoccupation with telephone calls and legal briefs, he opted not to bother asking her if she had enjoyed it. She was a tall, slender, elegant, statuesque woman with long, dark brown hair that she preferred to keep tucked up in a bun during the workday, since she said, like the horn-rimmed glasses, it made her look more professional. And although she discarded this attempted disguise when she came home, she often brought her work along with her. Tonight, even while she had eaten the chicken casserole, her head had remained buried in the paperwork pertaining to the case at hand. When Reginald asked about her day, the only response she gave was, "Fine."

As he went about clearing the table, rinsing the dishes, and placing them in the dishwasher, Ken's words reverberated in Reginald's mind. "Well, don't just stand there like a doddering old ninny!" he knew Ken would say, if he were here now. "Get started, already! Read the books I lent you!"

After doing the dishes, he started to read,

becoming so absorbed that he took the book to bed with him. Later, after they were both in bed, Reginald heard Eleanor say in a sleepy voice, "Reggie, darling, are you going to have the light on much longer?"

"I'm sorry," he said, "I just got caught up in this book by P. D. Ouspenski who …"

"I've got to be in court tomorrow, Reggie …" she interrupted him.

"Well, I can leave the reading for later if you want to …"

"Darling, I'd love to, but I can't tonight. I really need to get some sleep. Good night." And kissing him, she rolled over and buried her head in the pillow.

Reginald did not know whether to be relieved or disappointed. One thing was certain. If this was really the beginning of a new life, both he and Eleanor might be in for some shocks and rude awakenings. And could their marriage really endure the changes this new beginning would bring about?

3

Next morning Reginald fixed his wife an omelet, toast, and fruit cocktail for breakfast. While she ate, she was preoccupied with the organization of her paperwork and going over the details of her impending case. When she was ready to go, they exchanged a hasty kiss.

Reginald found himself alone. After a few minute's consideration, he dialed the office of Dean Archibald Shyster.

"Greetings, young man!" the dean said when he came on the line.

"Actually," Reginald replied dryly, "I'm sixty-five years old. I was calling to see if it was too late to enroll in the fall semester. I just retired as a professor of psychology at the University of Oklahoma and …"

"Say no more!" the dean shot back with all the enthusiasm of a used-car salesman. "We'd be happy to have you! Matter of fact, because of your age, we tend to waive certain requirements like transcripts and …"

"I've included all that information in my files," Reginald interrupted. "The only thing I need to draw up for you is a statement of purpose, and I'll have that by tonight. But I have to tell you, I'm Unitarian."

"No problem!" the dean assured him. "We pride ourselves on theological eclecticism! Tell you what. How'd you like to get together sometime soon for lunch, and I can show you around? I take it you got more under your belt than just the standard baccalaureate, as you've been a professor, did you say?"

"Yes," Reginald could feel energy being sapped from him.

"Say! Wait a minute. I was just looking over my itinerary. Seems I have an open spot tomorrow between eleven o'clock and three. Why don't we get together and I'll show you around the campus... talk over what we have to offer here. What do you say? If you have the credentials you say you have, we might even be able to qualify you for a scholarship of sorts!"

At this point, Reginald felt himself being hustled. He hated being hustled. "There's no need for financial assistance," he said.. "I've already got more than enough money to cover the costs. But I will take you up on your invitation."

When the conversation concluded soon after that, Reginald shook his head, partly in disbelief, and partly in sheer disgust. "What a turnoff," he muttered. "Ken was right. All you have to do is to hear that joker's voice to know he's a real bullshit artist."

Settling at his typewriter, Reginald began to compose his statement of purpose, all the while reminding himself that he could be a pretty good bullshit artist himself when the need presented itself. And a bullshitter trying to bullshit another bullshitter is pure bullshit.

Reginald spent the rest of the afternoon composing his statement of purpose. He wrote of his professional background, his years in the Unitarian church, and his more recent concern with the addressing of matters transcendent, including all the theological and Biblical details that he knew would make an impression, in a word, laying it on thick. "There!" he said. "This ought to let the ol' Shyster know he's not playing with some pimple-faced freshman. You play games with ol' Reggie Dexter, you play with dynamite!" And he let out a smug but hearty laugh. "I believe ol' Pastor Green's right," he muttered to himself. "This is going to be fun!"

Once again, that evening, Reginald fixed dinner for his wife and once again his wife appeared preoccupied with business matters.

"How'd it go in court today, Eleanor?" he asked finally.

"Pretty good," was Eleanor's response. "Have

to go back tomorrow. Cross-examinations, stuff like that. Going to have to do some more preparation. Got to give the client his money's worth. How was your day?" There was a rigid note of fixation in her voice that gave him a sense of her unbending single-mindedness.

Succumbing to a fit of resentment for being ignored, he said, "Oh, great! I'm going back to school in the fall to study to become the minister for the local Unitarian church. I'm also taking up tai chi, skydiving, and dirt biking, and a little bungee jumping."

"Retirement must be kind of boring, huh?" Eleanor said, clearly not hearing a word that he'd said. "Well, maybe in a few weeks, I can get away and we can do something together."

Resentment gave way to melancholy. That evening, while his wife poured over legal briefs, Reginald retired to the den and continued to read *"Zen and the Art of Motorcycled Maintenance."* Maybe, he thought, he'd buy himself a motorcycle too. Then he could pretend to be Steve McQueen.

The following morning, after again fixing Eleanor's breakfast and seeing her off to work, Reginald readied himself for the one-hundred-and-fifty-mile journey that lay ahead of him.

The hustle and rush of the city commute gave way to a pastoral display of rolling hills, farm fields, and small towns. The wind blew briskly through the trees, giving relief from the 89 percent humidity of the morning. Three and a half hours passed before Reginald finally arrived in the town of Idle, where he stopped at a gas station and asked directions to the university.

"The best advice I can give you is to stay away," the older of the two men sitting out front told him. "That place has so much of the devil in it, you can see sparks fly from a distance. Damn bunch of liberals. Heretics! That's what they are. Gonna lead us all into Hell, if they have their way!"

"Actually, it's straight up that hill," said the younger man.

"Yeah," said the old man, "straight up the hill and down to the pit! Bunch of communists. What denomination you lean toward?"

"I'm Unitarian." Reginald said.

"A-ha!" the old man shouted triumphantly. "I'm bettin' you're one of them!"

"I hate to have to tell you this," Reginald said, "but I believe there's a sharp contrast between Ralph Waldo Emerson and Karl Marx. Much as I'd like to continue our chat, I have an appointment to keep."

The younger man raised his can of soda in a mock toast. "Anytime, old timer," he said cheerfully. "Anytime."

As Reginald returned to his car, he thought to

himself, *I wonder if encounters such as these are a preview of the next three years.*

4

In comparison to the University of Oklahoma, the campus was miniscule. There could not have been more than twelve buildings, all models of turn-of-the-century American architecture made of red brick and mortar. They were, for the most part, single-story, varying in size, and rectangular. The newer buildings, such as the admissions and records office and the student center differed from the older ones only in that they were built of newer bricks.

Student traffic, although a lot sparser than at the University of Oklahoma was, Reginald would discover later, at its peak. It was a sultry day, but Reginald could not help but be taken aback by the students' state of undress, particularly the women, many of whom paraded around in particularly revealing halter tops and short blue-jean cutoffs. The males, many of them heading for class without shirts, weren't much better off. "Students aren't this immodest at O.U.," Reginald mumbled to himself, "and we're a secular university."

Consulting the map of the campus, he identified the student center to his left, along with the admissions and records office. Beyond these two structures were the classrooms and faculty offices scattered in a row on both sides of a cobblestone path that led up to the giant neoclassical seminary building that dominated the campus.

It was one minute to the hour when Reginald, who took pride in being prompt, arrived at the dean's office. The receptionist, a pert, red-haired, slender woman in her late thirties, greeted him cordially enough and buzzed Dr. Shyster, who wasted no time in coming out of his inner office. He was a diminutive man with a trim build and a receding hairline. His demeanor was bright and sanguine and his smile held great vitality. "Dr. Dexter!" he exclaimed, grasping Reginald's hand. "I've been looking forward to meeting you all morning. After what you told me over the phone about yourself, I can say most assuredly that you are going to be a welcome addition to the student body here at the seminary. It's very rare that we get someone of your caliber, your high degree of expertise, and ..."

"My transcripts," Reginald said dryly, passing him a manila envelope.

"Oh, sure, sure! No problem." He slid the contents out onto the secretary's desk and began to look them over. "Wow! Have you ever got credentials! And this statement of purpose! I'm going to need to sit down somewhere to read it. I expect it's a brilliant piece of work."

Either that or a piece of sheer bullshit, Reginald thought. "Look," he said. "I know this is rather late notice, but I was wondering if I still have a chance of getting into the fall semester?"

"No problem!" the dean assured him. "You're in! Look, why don't I show you around the place."

Dr. Shyster's abrupt willingness to accept Reginald left him baffled. During his years as a member of a university faculty, he had become quite familiar with the protocol that accompanied the acceptance process and he knew that it was customary, no matter what the circumstances, to adhere to standard procedure. Reginald recalled Ken saying that Dr. Shyster was always desperate for students, but Reginald expected at least some degree of examination, if only for purposes of maintaining a façade of academic standards.

"After going over your curriculum, I've elected to try combining my own field of expertise with theology," he explained when there was a momentary pause in the dean's panegyrics. "My concern is whether or not your library is adequately equipped for the task. Mind if I take a look at your resources?"

"Um, no problem," Dr. Shyster replied. "But we do assist our students in research by insisting they take a course their first semester here at the seminary that appropriately introduces them to utilizing a seminary library."

"That won't be necessary in my case, Dr. Shyster, "Reginald responded. "After forty years of doing research to meet with the University's 'publish or perish' policy, if there's one thing I've learned, it's my way around a library. The only thing I'm concerned with is the extent of your resources."

"Uh, Dr. Dexter," Dr. Shyster said, "every student in the seminary is required to take the library course. We can't just go around making exceptions."

"You will in my case," Reginald assured him.

Dr. Shyster was at a loss for words. "Sure," he said, proceeding to lead Reginald up the staircase to the library.

Reginald declined introduction to the seminary librarian and proceeded to immerse himself in the reference collection with Dr. Shyster close at hand. "I see you still use the Dewey Decimal System for classification purposes," he observed, refraining from adding that this meant that their collection was so small that the Library of Congress method wasn't even warranted. "Let's take a look at your psychology collection."

For the next hour, Reginald browsed the entire library collection, carefully scrutinizing every category, every subject heading and subheading, all the while making observations that clearly both awed and baffled his guide.

"About that library course," the dean said finally. "I believe, in your case, we can make an exception."

"Thank you," Reginald replied. "But I'd also like to take a look at the undergraduate library."

Over an hour passed as Reginald roamed from one section of the undergraduate library to another, leaving his now-frustrated host winded with the task of keeping up with him. Near the end of Reginald's in-depth examination of the library offerings, Reginald turned to his host and declared, "Well, Dr. Shyster, I'll be honest with you. Your libraries' holdings will not be adequate to meet my needs given the type of research I was planning on doing in conjunction with your curriculum. But I believe I can work around it. I still have library privileges at the University of Oklahoma, so what I can't get here, I'll get there. It's just a matter of planning things out properly."

"Hmmm," Dr. Shyster replied. "Say, Dr. Dexter! I don't know about you, but I'm getting a few hunger pangs. Why don't we check out the cafeteria? The food there is delicious, and it'll give me the opportunity to show you the dormitory guest quarters. I know they'll be ideal for you—it would make the most sense for you to stay there, since you plan to only be here three days a week."

"Sounds good. Lead the way."

On their way to the cafeteria to get something to eat, they stopped to look at the room where Reginald would stay, guest quarters that consisted of the only room in the dormitory that was carpeted. Reginald took note of the furnishings, assessing such items as electrical outlets, ventilation, and windows. It was also the only room in the dormitory, the dean admitted, that had curtains on the windows and linen on the beds, albeit the curtains were worn and the linen was minimal.

"I take it I'll have to supply my own lamps?" Reginald queried, "Well, it's a bit Spartan, but I suppose I can adjust." Reginald was reminded of a time long ago when, as an undergraduate and graduate student, he had endured the rigors of dormitory life — the noises of fellow students, the late-night boisterousness, and the sleep deprivation. At first, getting out from under parental dominion had been exciting, but it soon became old. He had been young then, too, and able to endure a great deal of inconvenience. Now, he found himself wondering if he really had the stamina and inclination to adjust again. Perhaps, he consoled himself; it would make him appreciate the luxuries of home all the more.

The cafeteria was furnished with row upon row of elongated dining tables that could accommodate a large number of students, although at the time of

Reginald's and Dr. Shyster's arrival, few of them were around, it being nearly 2 PM, Reginald's first bite of a rare roast beef sandwich came as a happy surprise. It seemed that the dean had been right in his claim of culinary excellence. "The food here is even better than the food at the U of O," Reginald said. "Is it always this good?"

"Yes!" Dr. Shyster responded. "It sure is."

At the same time, a student could be heard to say, "Ya know, the food here sure has been good this past week. Not like the crap they served us during the rest of the year. I wonder why the change all of a sudden."

"Don't you get it?" the other student told him. "It's graduation week. They're only doing it to suck up to our parents. It's their way of getting alumni to contribute more cash to their association."

Dr. Shyster blushed, desperately trying to maintain his dignity.

One thing he had to say in his favor, Reginald thought. He was certainly consistent. He didn't know if the dean was the biggest horse's ass he'd ever met in his life, but he certainly ranked in the top ten.

Later, after Dr. Shyster had signed the necessary paperwork admitting Reginald as a student, he shook his hand, and, grinning broadly welcomed him aboard, to which Reginald replied,

"Thanks, I think."

So, after completing the paperwork and paying the necessary fees at the Admissions and Records office, Reginald took his departure, which he commemorated by repeating Bette Davis's immortal words, "'What a dump.'"

5

Later that week, Reginald paid a visit to Ken Green, arriving late in the morning with the armload full of the books Ken had lent him. Some of them he found interesting, others excessively boring and tedious, St. Augustine's *City of God* being the worst of the lot. But he enjoyed the Zen books immeasurably. As a result, Reginald figured it was now time to render an update on his activities. Perhaps his friend might wish to extend some further insight with regards to his journey into a fruitful retirement.

Pastor Green was quick to answer his knock dressed in his usual casual attire consisting of corduroy trousers, a blue-striped polyester shirt, cardigan sweater and sandals.

"Come in! Come in!" Ken said. "Looks like you've got a real armload. Does this mean you've read all these since we last talked?"

Reginald set the books down on the coffee table. "It does," he replied. "When you've got as much free time on your hands as I do, keeping busy is the only way to maintain your sanity."

"And have you looked into enrollment at the

seminary?"

"I have. That was way too easy."

"I take it you met the dean. What did you think of ol' Shyster?"

"He was just like you said he'd be, only more so."

"Yep, a leopard like him doesn't change his spots too easily. But when you consider what he's got to contend with, it's understandable. That entire place has been a sinking ship for years. But, with skilled management and the right amount of hustle, they might be able to keep it afloat well into the eighties, which will mean you have more than enough time to get your credentials."

"Sounds like there might be a bit of scholastic erosion taking place," Reginald suggested. "Even now, I see compromised educational standards, administrative integrity going on the fritz, and I'll bet there might even be some questionable accounting practices…"

"Now, Reggie," Ken replied as he placed his hand on his friend's shoulder, "after all this time, you ought to know how much the academic world can prostitute itself. Matter of fact, I'm certain that, when the time is right, Dr. Shyster will jump ship and claim God's calling in doing so. What about the tai chi?"

"I checked into it, but the earliest class doesn't

start for another three weeks."

Ken shrugged, "Well, I'm pretty knowledgeable in the discipline. Why don't I get you started? You'll be able to get a jump on the class; you can begin your conditioning, and know what you're getting into, as well."

"Sound good," Reginald agreed. "Let's get started."

"Okay," Ken said, positioning himself, "Remember, if you incorporate this into your regular exercise program, you'll most likely experience an enhancement in energy and focus. But before we get started, I think it would be best if I went over a few things with you. Tai chi, or t'ai chi ch'uan, blends the features of healing, martial arts and meditation. The true focus of the study is on the mental and energetic levels, two features you'll find yourself desperately needing if you're going to be a student again. I'll bet it's been a long time since you've been a student. Now, listen up. You're going to need this, considering that most of your student colleagues will be somewhere between thirty-five and forty years your junior.

"The mental component will be your most important feature due to the fact that, without constant attention, we become very weak-minded, and being weak-minded means being easily confused and distracted," the pastor continued. "The need for focus is very important, and tai chi will help you maintain that. So, the first quality we need to develop in tai chi is the strengthening of your concentration. This is what the martial arts refer to as 'being centered,' which entails being in the present moment. So, with that in mind, let me introduce you to the beginning exercises. Better take off your coat; this is going to take awhile."

During that session, which lasted for an hour, Pastor Ken ran Reginald through some of the more rudimentary tai chi moves, which he attempted to commit to memory.

"Now I've given you quite a bit of material," his friend said when they had finished. "You might not be able to remember it all, and you might not be able to remember precisely how everything was done, but don't worry about it. The important thing is that you work at it twice a day on a regular basis. I'll see you in five days."

"By the way, Reggie, how's the missus?"

"Busy with a court case. What can I say?" Reginald said, slipping on his jacket. Actually, he could have said a good bit more, but much as he liked Pastor Ken, he had quite enough of him for one day.

6

That evening, Reginald put out the good dinner mats and crystal china on the dining room table. He thought of also arranging a centerpiece, but he figured that would probably just be wasted effort, since even though he had made a special effort, she would probably not notice. And he was right. Eleanor never took her eyes off the briefs during the meal, pouring over every word with an intensity that a brain surgeon might have applied to the removal of a tumor. Only after he had cleaned up the kitchen and begun his tai chi exercises was her concentration temporarily interrupted.

"Reggie," she said, "what on earth are you doing?"

His response did not appear to reassure her.

"Reggie, darling," she said. "Is this the first stage of senile dementia?"

Eleanor, he thought, had always had a sharp tongue, and sometimes she went too far.

"No, love," he said with admirable restraint. "Remember? I told you I had plans for doing other things. You know I've never been the type to, as Dylan Thomas would put it, 'go gentle into that good night.'"

"I think we need to get away together as soon as this case is over," she said, eyeing him pensively. "I think you need a change of scene. And for heaven's sake, if you intend to continue to take those odd positions, would you please do it somewhere else?"

She had, Reginald reflected as he made his way to the den, always been remarkably forthright. It occurred to him now that that particular attribute might not be quite the virtue he had always thought of it as being.

7

As the days passed, Reginald incorporated the tai chi moves into his exercise routine. Pastor Ken had given him more moves to work on after five days, and he was delighted to discover that those more rigorous exercises served to hone his sense of balance, as well as promote higher levels of energy, the likes of which he had not experienced for many years.

The tai chi classes themselves took place at the community center near Reginald's house, in a room decked out like a dojo with a red-rubber mat covering the floor and an instructor of Asian descent with a deep Louisiana drawl, garbed in an outfit resembling a white kimono.

Reginald performed so well that Mr. Chang congratulated him, but when he practiced at home, as he did every evening while Eleanor poured over legal briefs, he heard her say once, after glancing up at him, "I think senility is beginning to take hold."

And yet, despite what sounded like mockery, she turned to him in bed that night and they found themselves caught up in surprisingly torrid lovemaking that continued into the wee hours of the morning.

Winded and exhilarated from the experience, Eleanor noted Reginald grinning broadly, surprisingly composed, and breathing gently. "Reggie," she said, "where'd you learn to make love live that?"

"What do you mean 'like that,' love?" Reginald asked, inwardly still grinning.

"You know perfectly well what I mean, Reggie. In all the years we've been married, you've never made love to me like *that* before, and I want to know what brought about the change."

"You were one factor that brought about the change — a beautiful, seductive temptress that could lead astray the most saintly of men. Fortunately, I'm the lucky one who has a license to be lead astray," Reginald responded. And, Reginald thought, those tai chi exercises and the notion of summoning my chi could be applied to a number of things. Maybe that's why Asia is so overpopulated.

"Oh, Reggie," Eleanor said embracing him, "I think I'll keep you."

Reginald took the words as a confirmation of Pastor Ken's human recycling program. He was sure now that he would not go gentle into that good night. But his work had just begun.

8

"Well done! I believe the time has come for your next step," Pastor Ken said when, the next day, Reginald recounted his success of the night before. "Now, it's time to take a stab at skydiving."

Reginald's face turned rapidly from a jubilant red to a ghastly pale. "Look, Ken," he said, "I have to level with you … I can't do that. The very thought of falling scares me to death, let alone jumping out of a plane."

"But we can't let our fears dictate our actions," Pastor Ken admonished him.

"Well, it won't!" Reginald declared firmly, "because in my case, it's going to be an *inaction*."

"Now, Reggie," Pastor Ken soothed him, "it's only natural for you to be somewhat scared."

"Terrified is more the word," Reginald corrected him. "Look, I aspired to be a paratrooper during World War II, but back then, I was young and stupid. I thought I was invulnerable. I happen to know better now. Besides, the army had more sense than to allow me to do that back then. It's thirty-some years later now, and I'm not about to do now what the Army didn't allow me to do. The Army probably had more sense than me."

"Can't you see? That's the very reason you should go through with this," Pastor Ken told him. "Your fear, and everyone else's for that matter, is nature's way of forcing us to acknowledge and respect danger. But sometimes that fear only gets in the way of what we need to do and what we need to be. It also produces inappropriate reactions for the occasion. For instance, ever been in an automobile accident? For the sake of illustration, suppose, one day on the road, you were confronted with a situation that might result in a collision. What steps do you feel you could take to avoid that?"

Reginald returned his gaze. "Well, I guess I could slam on the brakes with the hope of stopping the car before impact," Reginald suggested, aware that this might not be the sort of comprehensive response his friend sought to elicit.

"Did you know that pumping the brakes would stop you more quickly?" Pastor Ken said. "But that would hardly be the reaction of the average person on the road. Most people would either do what you did, and turn the wheel 180 degrees, thereby going into a skid, or do nothing, or simply brace themselves for the impact. But all the while, the best way to address the situation is simply to turn the wheel slightly, or pump the brakes effortlessly. My point here is this: as long as you acknowledge your fear and respect danger, you should be able to overcome the fears you have. Knowing what to do in certain situations can also be helpful. And if you overcome these fears, your life will become so much more enjoyable. And if you think the sex you had last night was great, you're just beginning to cross the threshold!"

Pastor Ken placed one hand on Reginald's shoulder, "There's no reason that you shouldn't enjoy life more, the older you get," he said. "But you can't let yourself be afraid to try anything. Go home. Do your tai chi. Make your wife happy. And tomorrow get your middle-aged butt out onto that airfield and face that fear of yours head on—and defeat it!"

Pastor Ken's words were rich with an authority that Reginald did not allow himself to resist. He drew in their wisdom and, with resolve, departed to begin preparation for what lay ahead. The next day found him driving to Cushing Municipal Airport, his stomach tied in knots. With great misgivings he entered the building where a burly man in his mid-thirties with luxurious locks of thick, black, long wavy hair said, "Help ya, mister?"

"Is this where I learn about skydiving?"

"Hey," the man replied, "what's an old codger like you want with skydiving? Wouldn't golf be more suitable? I mean, we don't get too many seniors with the desire to learn this stuff. And if you've got some sort of death wish, I'm warning ya, we don't want any of that here, either! We got a reputation to look after!"

"No, no!" Reginald protested. "It's nothing like that! I really want to learn to skydive."

"Why?" Was the abrupt response.

"Because I never had the experience before, and it's something I'd like to try!"

"Let me guess. Retirement's boring."

"That's part of it," Reginald admitted, already feeling cowed.

"Well, if that's what you want, that's what we're here for." He reached for some paperwork on the counter. "You'll start out with a tandem dive. But before that, you'll need to take part in a forty-five minute ground-school orientation class. Here's some paperwork for you to fill out. The next class is in an hour." Pausing to gaze thoughtfully at Reginald a few moments, he then added, "Ya know, we've had people go ballistic on us and they weren't even half your age."

His words were not the soothing assurance Reginald needed at this time. He was still trying to replay Ken's words in his mind, but he could not hear them over the rapid pounding of his heart and the dizzying, panicky buzz in his ears. When the man handed Reginald the papers. Reginald looked them over carefully. Let's see, he thought. Sign here. Initial there. Yes, I agree to sign my life away. Might as well since that's what I'm doing. Okay. Yes, I acknowledge the school is in no way responsible for anything (initial), anytime (initial), anywhere (initial). Sign here. No, I will not attempt to sue. Initial here. How can I sue if I'm dead? Of course, my wife's an attorney. She didn't agree not to sue. And if she knew what I was doing now, she'd probably want to kill me. Okay. Print here. Sign there. Reginald then remembered a hymn he was taught during his childhood and vaguely mouthed its lyrics as he waited. "Nearer my God to thee, nearer to thee…"

The ground-school class lasted a bit over the allotted forty-five minutes due to the number of questions asked regarding the procedure. At the last minute, two members of the class decided not to make the jump and Reginald was tempted to make it a threesome. However, in the end, he joined the others boarding the flight, partially reassured by the fact that he would make the jump with an instructor strapped to his back, both of them buoyed by a single large parachute.

Seated on a bench in the converted cargo plane, as it sped down the runway on its way to the prescribed height of 14,000 feet, Reginald looked over at the rest of the jumpers, all garbed, like him, in gray flight suits with parachutes strapped to their backs. One woman, a lady in her mid-forties with auburn hair and medium build, appeared beside herself with fright. Meanwhile, a man, about six foot, four inches and in his early twenties, appeared as eager as a school kid. In each instance, their instructors responded to them accordingly, one trying to bolster the lady's courage, the other trying to calm the man down and dissuade his impulsiveness.

Reginald reflected on what he was told in the orientation class. There were two cords to pull. If one did not open the chute, then he was to pull the other. He turned to check their location. He was, he knew, to extend his arms outward, a directive that went counter to his first impulse, which was to keep his hands as close to the cords as possible. He looked over at his flight instructor, a young woman who looked strangely familiar.

"Say," he said, "didn't I have you in one of my classes?"

"I believe you did," she replied, smiling. "Actually, Professor Dexter, I've read everything you've written, in fact. I'm Marlene Rogers. I'm a graduate psych student at O.U. This is how I work my way through college. Never expected to see you here, even though I did have you pegged for being a bit on the eccentric side."

"How about totally insane?"

"Well, now that you mention it and seeing that you're here right now... but don't worry, I've done this hundreds of times, and I'm gonna get you through this one, trust me. It'll be fun!" She then reached for the fasteners. "It's going to be our turn to jump soon, so let's get fastened."

Reginald drew a bit of reassurance from Marlene's experience, although not enough to keep his breathing from constricting. His thoughts again returned to World War II, and the time when he originally aspired to be a paratrooper, only to be denied the opportunity. He had never been told what it was that made him unsuitable. And then he found himself remembering the voice of President Franklin Delano Roosevelt stating that the only thing we had to fear was fear itself. Roosevelt had been right, of course, and the army had been wrong. And now he had a chance to prove it.

"C'mon, Dr. Dexter! It's time to go!" Marlene cried, awakening him from the troubling memories.

Reginald rose to his feet and together they moved in sync toward the plane's exit. "Okay, Professor Dexter," Marlene yelled. "We're all set!" Reginald glanced out the exit and could feel the wind rushing by. Again he felt his breathing constrict and his heart pounded hard and rapidly. Before he could entertain another thought, he heard

Marlene's voice yell from behind him, "Okay, ready, set …"

"Go" was supposed to be the next word, but Reginald did not hear it. All he heard was the rush of the wind as both he and Marlene flung themselves out the door. This was, he realized, the sound of falling 120 miles per hour straight down. When Marlene then gave Reginald the signal, "arms out." he was dumbfounded to find that he was actually doing this. Not that he was comfortable. On top of everything else, the parachute straps felt like they were about to cut him in half. His lungs had no room to expand. But surprisingly, he had no sensation of falling. There he was, suspended in space, hanging there with the earth apparently miles away. As Marlene's fist flew into his face, he knew it was time to pull the cord. Where SWOOSH … JERK …and then silence as the parachute dropped them slowly, 1,000 feet to land with an impact comparable to jumping off a one-story building, depositing them safely in a grassy field three-hundred yards from the airfield.

Reginald got to his feet dumbfounded. He couldn't believe he had just done what he had, and survived. The parachute tangled about them as they slowly and meticulously worked to gather in the chute. Just as the gathering process was about completed, a truck came by to transport them back to the airfield. "You did very well for your first time out!" Marlene exclaimed. "And for someone as old as you, I can't help but be impressed by your courage! Want to try it again?"

"I'll have to think about it," Reginald told her, sighing with relief. But it had been exhilarating. In fact, he had felt a rush of adrenaline the likes of which he had never felt before. He also felt he had experienced a bit of what it was like to die. And while attaining a glimpse his own death, fear itself had died with it.

That night, while he fixed dinner, Eleanor recounted how difficult the day was for her in court and how exhausted she was, going on to good-naturedly blame Reginald for their late night. After her complaints had been sufficiently aired, she insisted on another session. Reginald obliged. Pastor Ken was right again. It was even better than the night before.

"I love you now more than ever, Reggie." she sighed, as he cradled her in his arms. "Am I really that much of an inspiration to you?"

Reginald decided not to tell her about his aerial exploits. Somehow it didn't seem like the appropriate time.

9

Reginald went on a half a dozen more tandem skydiving ventures, impressing Marlene Rogers with the way he handled himself so much that it was not long before she certified him for a solo jump. And so it was that, one day, he found himself standing in the doorway of the plane, this time without the backup of a flight instructor, longing for the freedom of flight. Leaping upward and outward, he could feel the force of the wind as it supported him, fighting against the pull of gravity, holding him at a constant speed when he extended his arms and touched nothing but air. He was aware of an exhilarating inner rush of adrenaline. And although he was soaring through the sky at 120 miles per hour, he felt himself in total control. The slightest movement of his body could, he found, alter his speed, his heading, and his position. Yet, the newly acquired thrill of danger sharpened his focus, heightened his senses, and slowed down the passage of time. He felt extremely alive. Every nerve in his body tingled with excitement. It was, he thought, the second greatest experience anyone could have in this life.

The earth, with its colors variegated, was the

place he lived. Yet it was in the sky where he felt most alive. For sixty seconds out of the span of an eternity, Reginald felt a new sense of freedom from all worldly concerns. For those sixty seconds, the only things that existed were himself and the sky.

According to his altimeter, Reginald was one mile above the earth that was fast rising up to meet him. When he reached the four-thousand-feet mark, the earth seemed to expand. And when, after another five seconds elapsed and he had a scant three thousand feet left in his fall, he reached for the cord and opened up his life-saving parachute, the mad rush of wind quickly transformed into a peaceful calm that lasted until the pull of gravity began to reassert itself.

Now, as he sank below the two hundred foot mark, the earth became like a leviathan, ready to swallow him whole. At twelve feet he pulled the toggles and slowed his descent to end gently in a field, and met by a flushed and enthusiastic Marlene who ran to greet him.

That evening, Reginald was home again in time to fix his wife a scrumptious candlelight dinner complete with an exotic recipe acquired years prior during a trip he had taken to France with members of his fraternity. He was quite meticulous in his selection of wine as Johnny Mathis crooned on the stereo.

He heard her car pulling into the driveway. He reached for the switch on the wall and dimmed the lights. Reginald's timing was, as usual, impeccable. All preparations were complete as Eleanor entered the front door. Reginald walked over and kissed her cheek as she entered. "Welcome home, my darling," he said. "May I take your coat?"

"Oh, dear!" she exclaimed. "I wasn't expecting this! I mean really, Reggie…"

Reginald silently removed her jacket, walked to the other side of the dining room and hung it up in the closet, then walked over to the cabinet adjacent to the closet. He opened the cabinet door and pulled out a bottle of wine and two glasses. "Would you like to partake of a little wine before dinner?" He handed her a glass and poured the wine into it.

Eleanor stared at Reginald, a bit overwhelmed. "Reggie, darling, what has gotten into you lately?"

Reggie slipped his arms around Eleanor's waist from behind and began to caress her. "Mmm, my love," he said. "What's gotten into me must be my getting into you."

"I see," she said slyly. "And I suppose this wine is meant to break down my resistance?"

"I sincerely hope so."

"Reggie, darling," she said, gently pushing him away, "I entered this marriage with you years ago with my eyes wide open. I knew there might be problems later on, because of the wide gap in our ages. But these past few weeks, I have seen behavior from you that I am totally unprepared for, and I have to tell you that I'm at a loss as to what to make of it."

"What might that behavior be? Are you troubled, my love?"

Again, she spoke with care as her eyes fixed squarely upon Reginald. "To be quite truthful, Reggie, darling, yes I am!" she exclaimed. "Ever since your retirement, you've become obsessively involved with your tai chi, not to mention becoming sexually insatiable. I've also had the nagging feeling you're doing things you haven't told me about."

Reginald smiled. "Guilty on all counts, my love, except that I did tell you once that I wanted to try skydiving, dirt bike riding, bungee jumping, and hang gliding. Of course, at the time I made the announcement, you were absorbed in a court case."

"Skydiving?" she cried. "Hang gliding? All right, Reggie, I'll admit some of this has been my fault, but as your wife, I believe I have the right to know what's going on with you, especially if you're risking your life!"

"Well, first off," Reginald told her, feeling suddenly embarrassed, "I want to be important to you again."

"You *are* important to me!" Eleanor responded

as she reached out to embrace him again. "You've *always* been important to me. You're my lifetime partner, and nothing's going to change that!"

Reginald's voice assumed a grim note of determination as he looked Eleanor squarely in the eye. "Secondly, *nobody* is throwing old Reginald Dexter on life's scrap heap until he's ready to go! If they won't let me teach anymore at the University, by God I'll do something else. I may be over-the-hill chronologically, but I've still got a lot of mileage left in me. Maybe another fifty years. Maybe more! And those years are going to be dynamic ones! The world's going to see that Reginald Dexter is a man to be reckoned with!"

"We need to talk," said Eleanor. It was a good talk, and Eleanor was surprisingly understanding when he told her everything that he had been doing since retirement. In fact, he saw a look of admiration in her eyes, and she didn't turn a hair when he told her that, come the fall, she would have to fend for herself for three days during the week, at least. But she was uneasy about the bungee jumping, the dirt bike riding, and the hang gliding. He could see that. "Those are dangerous activities," she said emphatically, "and I'd like to keep you around for awhile."

"You still don't understand, my love," he said, "I'm doing this so I *will* stay around!"

"Are you planning on doing another jump?"

"Yes."

"When?"

"Saturday."

"I'm coming with you, then."

"You are?" Reginald froze in mid-stretch and sat upright with surprise in his voice.

"Sure," she replied, smiling gently. "What makes you think you've got the right to be the only crazy one in this marriage?"

10

The following Saturday, when Eleanor joined Reginald on the trip to the airport, it was clear that his reassurances about what Pastor Ken had said did little to quiet her fears.

Once inside the airfield's hangar, Reginald spotted Marlene Rogers over by the counter where the parachutes were stored.

"Eleanor, this is Marlene Rogers, a one-time student of mine," he said, "and also my mentor in skydiving. She's the one who certified me to jump solo." He then turned his focus to Marlene. "I've told my wife, Eleanor, about my activities here at the airfield, and now she wants to go skydiving with me."

"How romantic," Marlene said, smiling effervescently. "I wish my boyfriend would go skydiving with me, but he's afraid of heights. The big sissy."

"Sounds to me like your boyfriend has a lot of good sense," Eleanor told her.

Reginald grinned a sheepish grin. "I was wondering," he said, "could Eleanor and I take a tandem jump?"

"Well, it's not what we generally recommend, but given the fact that you've become so expert at this, I see no problem," Marlene replied. "Of course, you'll both need to sit through the orientation class."

"No problem," Reginald replied.

"Yes, no problem at all," Eleanor chimed in. She was really in no hurry to get on the plane.

Less than an hour later, flight suits were donned, parachutes were issued, and soon Eleanor and Reginald were in line to board the plane. Eleanor, who appeared more than just a little shaken, said suddenly taking his arm, "Reggie, I don't think this is a very good idea."

"Of course, it's a good idea," he replied with a chuckle. "Trust me, darling, you'll love it. Just follow my lead. I guarantee, it'll be like nothing you've ever experienced before."

"That's what I'm afraid of."

"You know, in many ways, you remind me of me just a few weeks ago," he told her reassuringly. "I almost didn't make that jump. But now I can say in all earnestness that it was the best thing I ever did. Well … maybe not the *best* thing I've ever done. That may have to wait until we get home tonight."

"Now, Reggie," she said, "are you absolutely sure that one of these cords will open up the chute?"

"You heard what the flight instructor said," he told her. "If they don't, we can take the next jump absolutely free of charge."

"Ha ha," she replied. "This is a hell of a time for humor."

"That's another thing an activity like this will do," he told her, grinning. "It will improve your sense of humor."

They soon found themselves seated on the plane. A chill rushed through Eleanor as she felt the plane begin to taxi down the runway. The chill accentuated itself all the more as she felt the plane leave the ground and gain altitude quickly.

Reginald moved in closer to Eleanor and said, "Well, love, it's about that time," Reginald said when they had reached 14,000 feet. "Let's strap ourselves together."

Eleanor's voice was trembling, as was her entire body. "Reggie," she cried, "I can't."

"Oh, sure you can, love," Reggie replied. "I'm right here beside you, and I'll get you through this. Trust me. You'll be glad you did. It's time to get in line before they open the door. Come on, darling. It's just like rolling off a log."

"Aren't you the one for questionable analogies."

"Remember your first time with sex?"

"Yeah, I was close to the ground, then," she reminded him. "It didn't happen at 14,000 feet. I can't do this. Don't you understand? Stop pulling me along with you! No! No!!"

Now, standing at the exit, Reggie hollered, "Okay, now's the time! Ready … Set. …"

And then they were plunging together through the air, and if Reginald had expected her to scream, he was disappointed. In fact, although it might have been the wind, he thought he heard her laugh. By the time the chute had opened and they had drifted into an open field, they were both laughing. And while still covered with silk, they began to kiss one another so passionately that Marlene, who uncovered them, said, "All right, you two lovebirds, you can resume this activity later. Right now, it's time to get untangled and into the truck."

Eleanor was first to find her voice. "Reggie," she said in a low voice, "I think I'm finally beginning to grasp what you've been trying to tell me of your retirement, and you know something? I believe you've been doing me a favor as well."

"And how might that be, my love?" Reginald asked.

"Why, isn't it obvious? You've been giving me a point of reference to follow once I hit my socially imposed 'old age.' You were right. God and I, not society, will decide when it's time for me to die."

"That's very profound, my love," Reginald replied.

"I also have a few regrets, as well," she

continued, "I've been so preoccupied with this damn court case that I've been too busy to be there for you during what might possibly have been the most traumatic adjustment of your life. But everything is going to change now. It's six weeks before your classes start, and I have a lot of vacation time. Let's get reacquainted. I believe you and I have some catching up to do!"

Which was precisely what they did, with the result that at the end of the summer, all he could say, as he prepared to leave for Idle was, "I don't want to lose you."

Eleanor gave him a flirtatious, yet reassuring look. "I'm not going anywhere."

TAKEN UP BEFORE
THE GENERAL

My name is Daryl MacGregor and I am an Army brat. This is the label I was born with, the tag that followed me throughout my childhood and adolescence, and perhaps, for most of my life.

Army life is a world that is carefully orchestrated, with outward conformity held at a premium. It is a world filled with Quonset huts, mess halls, reduced cost for whatever few recreational privileges are offered, commissaries, base exchanges, and consistently altering venues at the whims of the upper echelons. Families gather at the airport as Daddy parts company and flies toward potentially dangerous liaisons, perhaps never to return. The scenery changes at varying intervals of rapidity; you arrive in town, case the place, and just when you think you know your way around, it's time to leave. Friendships are, at best, transient. In many instances, the friends we have, at any given moment, become strangers again. It is a world in which you would expect families to cleave together. But under the shadow of the military's tyrannical dictates, family members oftentimes find themselves at a point of chaotic disengagement. Despite all this, it is a constricted world — and *this was my world.*

My father was a warrant officer, a curious rank to hold in the military's hierarchical scheme, sandwiched as it is between the commissioned and the noncommissioned officers. Those achieving this rank had access to all officer privileges, yet, despite their station, warrant officers associated with the enlisted ranks more often than would any commissioned officer. It had taken my father many years of diligent devotion to duty and extreme dedication to his military taskmaster to earn this rank, one frequently described as officers who were "mean as hell and twice as nasty," and "neither fish nor fowl." After all, the typical warrant officer worked his way up through the ranks from buck private and was still in the awkward position of being answerable to the institutionally tagged "ninety-day wonders" who achieved higher levels of rank and authority by way of a college degree and three months of officers' candidate school, officers my dad often referred to as "those punk lieutenants."

Father was the consummate military man. With the exception of his fatigues, his uniform was always sharply cleaned and pressed, every medal and insignia properly pinned in place, and his shoes meticulously shined. Father was possessed with every attribute you would ascribe to a "lifer" since, for over thirty years, it was the military that had sustained him. It was his master, his nurturer, his mistress, and his god, and he, in turn, was a man consumed with an almost symbiotic attachment to the organization, at the expense of wife, children, and even himself.

As nearly as I could ascertain from the people who knew him back in his early years, it was the military that had kept him from becoming a lost soul with a penchant for self-destruction, living a life that was going nowhere.

He cut his schooling short in the eleventh grade, feeling that it had nothing more to teach him. After leaving school, he had embarked on a series of jobs, from which he would either wind up quitting due to lack of compatibility with coworkers or be fired for insubordination. My father, so I have been told, was also cursed with a wild streak that caused him, occasionally, to run afoul of the local constabularies.

In the small Iowa town where her grew up, his exploits, which included, during the two years after he left school, public drunkenness, brawling, disorderly conduct, and creating a public nuisance, made him a well-known figure. Finally, in June of 1941, just scant months before the bombing of Pearl Harbor, he was called upon to serve his year of military conscription. America's entry into World War II extended his time of service, and his own propensities gave him cause to remain in the service until his forced retirement some thirty-one years later.

On many subsequent occasions, Father espoused the redemptive nature of the path he had chosen. "It was the military that straightened my ass out!" he would state emphatically. "And I think every man should be obligated to do at least one hitch in the service and serve his country! It's the price every man should pay for the privilege of living in America! It's what every boy needs to become a man!"

Naturally, this requisite did not exclude his son. He was inclined to relive his youth through me, despite the fact that we couldn't have been less alike. He viewed me as a wayward smart aleck whose self-willed nature was in desperate need of tempering, and would often say to me, "One day the military's going to draft your young ass! Then we'll see where you and that smart mouth of yours will wind up! And by God, I hope I'm around to see it!" It was a prediction that left me with a distinct sense of foreboding.

Living under his roof and placed within the confines of military settings for a good portion of my life, I felt consigned to a place just a tad worse than Hell, and shuddered at being predestined to fulfill his ideals. My smart-aleck demeanor and penchant for irony became crude coping mechanisms during the dawning of my adolescence; they salved the wounds brought about by life's frequent changes and the visions of Father's ominous dictums regarding my future. In many ways this mode of coping made me oblivious to pain and bereft of the capacity to mourn: I remember, many years later, attending Father's funeral and not shedding one tear.

Growing up, it appeared to me that the military, when it was not waging war, took on all the features of a theatrical presentation with carefully staged scenes, meticulously rehearsed lines, and tightly choreographed movements. Cues were rendered with precise timing and little room was given for improvisations. Of course, this manifested the obvious pomp and circumstance of formal rites and parades, but it also extended to the mundane. For example, attending the movie theater on base, before we could enjoy the movie, a certain ritual needed to be performed. Old Glory would unfurl across the screen, and we would all stand as the National Anthem was played. Only after this ritual had been completed could we all sit back and watch the film.

Once a minor glitch plagued this careful orchestration. We were all standing in place as the Stars and Stripes waved across the screen, when something went wrong with the sound system. Bereft of a proper cue, we remained standing, wondering what to do next. Fortunately, a uniformed officer was present. Stepping to the forefront of the theater, he led us all in the Pledge of Allegiance, after which, proper homage had been adequately paid, and we could all sit back and relax as the projectionist continued trying to repair the sound system.

I often wondered what would happen if someone dared to breach this theatrical façade and to this end, opted during the spring of my fifteenth year to test the boundaries. We were doing a three-year tour of Germany in Kaiserslautern at the time, living in base housing just on the outskirts of town. School had let out a few hours prior, and a short time before six, when retreat would be sounded; I was riding my bike around the shopping area. All traffic had stopped moving in preparation for the daily ritual, and everyone wearing a uniform was facing the flag, prepared to render a salute until Taps had concluded. If you were a non-uniformed entity, you were expected to stop what you were doing, face in the direction of the flag, and place your hand over your heart until the end of "Taps." It was another one of the military's theatrical rituals no one ever questioned.

I spent months planning my deviation from this practice, and today would be the day of its execution. The only question I entertained was, did I really have enough nerve to pull it off?

The moment finally arrived. "Taps" began to play, and, like the components in a well-honed machine, everyone about me ceased movement. Everyone turned and faced the flag. Uniformed personnel rendered a salute. Those not in uniform stopped and placed their hands over their hearts. As for me, I kept on riding my bicycle. Scant seconds passed when I heard an ear-shattering call.

"You! Biker!"

I turned and beheld a very young, immaculately uniformed soldier whose white arm-band declared him an M.P., heading in my direction.

"You know what time it is?" the soldier shouted.

I looked at my watch. "Six o'clock. Why?"

"Don't you know retreat is now sounding?"

"All I was doing was riding my bike," I replied realizing that my mouth had gone dry. "I'm not planning on attacking anything."

"Don't try getting cute with me, boy!" the soldier retorted roughly, coming to a stop directly in front of me. "When the trumpet sounds retreat you're suppose to get off your bike, face the flag, put your hand over your heart, and hold that salute until 'Taps' is finished playing! You got that?"

"But Sir," I responded, "I'm a Jehovah's Witness and …"

"I don't give a damn whose witness you are! When the trumpet sounds 'Taps,' you get off that bike of yours, place your hand over your heart, and you salute that fuckin' flag! Is that clear?"

"But, sir, according to my religious practice, I'm ...

"I don't want to hear about your goddamn religion! I'm telling you, if you wanna stay healthy, you better stop and salute that fuckin' flag when fuckin' 'Taps' is playin'! Is that fuckin' clear?"

"But sir, according to Exodus 20, verses four and five, 'You shall not make for yourself a graven image — any likeness of anything that is in Heaven above, or that is in the earth beneath or that is in the water under the earth; you shall not bow down to them nor serve them. For I, the Lord am a jealous God ...' So telling me to pay homage in such a manner would violate my ..."

"I don't give a good goddamn about your fuckin' religious beliefs or your fuckin' Bible!" he shouted.

"But sir, according to the third amendment in our Bill of Rights, we have the guarantee of freedom to live and practice our religious beliefs ..."

"I don't wanna hear any o' your Bill of Rights bullshit either! When eighteen-hundred hours rolls around, you get off that bike and salute that fuckin' flag!"

"Sir, am I to understand that you are denying me my constitutional rights?"

"You're goddamn right I'm denying you your Constitutional rights!"

"But, sir, even our president, your commander in chief, stated …"

"Oh, fuck the president!"

The conversation didn't last too much longer. I think both of us felt any further dialogue would be counter-productive. When he asked me for my name, and I explained that his insistence on my compliance to such a demand constituted a violation of my rights to privacy, he threatened to thrash me with his baton. Ultimately, I gave him my name. He issued me a citation. I got back on my bike and headed home.

At last, I knew what would happen if I breached the military's theatrical code of conduct. According to what my father told my mother, the citation reached the desk of Colonel Virgil Compton, my father's commanding officer, the next day, resulting in my father receiving a summons two days later.

"Mr. MacGregor …" the Colonel returned my father's salute. "Have a seat. As you probably already know, a citation was issued to your son for violation of procedural practices regarding retreat."

"No, I didn't know anything about it," my

father replied.

"Well," the Colonel said, "here's a copy of the report. Apparently, your son was trying to test the limits of post regulations. Nothing major, but I am required to issue you a reprimand. You know the drill. I place it in your file, and then expunge it six months later. But I would recommend keeping a tighter reign on your son's activities. You know how touchy top brass gets over violations such as these."

"Yes, sir."

"Although I can surmise, it's never easy … raising teenagers, that is."

"Tell me about it," Father responded with a forced grin.

"How old is your son?"

"Fifteen."

"Oh, yes. That's the age when they start developing their own personalities. And you just want to beat them within an inch of their lives because of it. My daughter's sixteen — stubborn as an ox and self-willed as sin itself — you wouldn't believe. I told her to stop dating the GI's, but I still think she's been cavorting with them behind my back. Well, anyway, that's all I had to talk with you about, Mr. MacGregor."

"Okay, sir." He then got up to leave. Just as he was about to reach the door, the Colonel called his name.

"Mr. MacGregor …"

"Yes, sir?"

"I meant to tell you… food service has really picked up since you've been assigned to this unit. Keep up the good work."

"Yes, sir. I will, sir. Thank you, sir."

This is what I overheard him tell my mother, but the report he gave me was a different thing entirely.

"Daryl!" I heard him yell.

"Yeah, Dad?" I replied.

"Don't you 'yeah Dad' me, ya little bastard!" He retorted angrily. "You see this? He waved a piece of paper in front of my face. "Read it! Just what the hell were you thinking when you pulled that shit-ass stunt? You know what I had to go through? I got called in by my CO and a reprimand is now in my file! And it's all because of a smart-ass punk teenager I have the misfortune to have as a son! And right now, I am ashamed to have to call you that!"

"Now, dear," my mother chimed in, "I don't think we need to …"

"Stay out of this!" he shouted. "This is between me and Daryl!" He turned back to me. "I got a reprimand in my file because of you! It's gonna be in my file for six months --- six fuckin' months! My spotless record is now blemished because of your stupid stunt. But if you think you're just gonna walk away from this incident scott-free, think again! As long as that reprimand remains in my file, you're grounded! You know what that means?"

Unfortunately I knew what that meant all too well, but I also knew that he intended to tell me.

"I'll tell you what that means!" he continued, answering his own question. "It means after school, every day for the next six months, you are to come directly home from school! No stopping at the stores on base, no riding your bike around, no sacking groceries at the commissary for tips, no lollygagging at the base teen club ... nothing! Nicht! Zip! Nada! You are to come straight home, do your homework, then go to bed. No TV! No comic books! No radio!" He paused for breath, and I noted that his face was an unusual shade of red. "By God, you're gonna know that shit rolls down hill, and if my ass is gonna be in a sling, I'm gonna see your ass in there right alongside mine! Now go to your room!"

At this juncture, my curiosity about breaches of theatrical protocol was more than satisfied. But my travails were far from over. The events of the days that were to follow were destined to acquaint me with further unpleasant realities.

The next day at school, in third period biology, I was re-reading a segment of the day's assignment when Michelle Tinzer appeared beside me. Michelle had gained the reputation of the sophomore class vamp, and with good reason. Miniskirts and other Carnaby Street apparel were in fashion back then, but wearing them was strictly forbidden by the high school dress code, all of which didn't seem to stop Michelle who always came to school garbed in attire provocative enough to guarantee that adolescent hormones would, at the very least, be stimulated.

I must have been a late bloomer back then, because despite all her efforts, I remained unfazed by her appearance. In fact, during the two years I had been attending the base school, word had gotten out that I had never been seen with a girl. A few students even referred to me as, "the campus fag." Of course, to Michelle, this was viewed as a challenge.

"Don't try to hide the truth from me, Daryl!" she said with coyness in her voice.

"What?" I said, looking up from my book.

"Always playing the innocent little boy, aren't you, Daryl? But you know what you did."

"Oh, shut up, Michelle!" I responded. "Please, shut up!"

"You fucked her, Daryl! You bad, bad boy! Now she's pregnant and you're gonna have to marry her!" Michelle said.

"Oh, shit!" I said. "This is getting old."

Just then another classmate approached me. He

was a tall, slender boy with black hair and freckles covering his face. "What's this I hear about Daryl getting some broad pregnant?" he said. "Is it true?" He then turned to face the rest of the class. "Hey! Daryl knocked up some broad!"

Pretty soon, the entire classroom was humming with jubilant banter, all attention centered on me. For the past three weeks, this tiresome spectacle had been standard fare, picking up momentum on a daily basis. Just two weeks prior, word of my alleged exploits had started leaking over into my other classes, and students that I didn't even know were approaching me with this gossip.

Up to now, I had brushed it off as being just another nuisance of the many I had had to deal with while attending this school. But today, things were destined to take a volatile turn for the worse.

At the conclusion of third period biology, as I was sorting through my books at my locker, Bill Rice, Kevin Songerman, along with their ring leader, John Crawford, three of the school's more renowned bully boys, approached me. John was about half-a-head taller than me with lanky hair and a look in his eyes that boded no good. He had been pursuing me for months, trying desperately to pick a fight with me for reasons I could not fathom.

Unbeknownst to me at the time, a certain unwritten code prevailed in this fortress setting that prescribed a process of initiation wherein the inductee was called out to fight. And fight he must. It didn't matter whether he won or lost; what mattered was that he was "man" enough to fight. Fighting was one aspect of teenage life I never wanted to take part in. Being the consummate coward, oftentimes I would go a mile or two out of my way to avoid it. This, however, made John and company more determined.

"Hey, prickhead!" he said, pushing me hard against the locker. "Today's the day! I'm calling you out!"

I felt highly imposed upon for having to deal with this now. I also felt a twinge of fear in the pit of my stomach, which, no doubt my expression betrayed. "What for?" I asked.

"'Cause you're a spineless, gutless, sissified fairy, that's why!"

"Then why do you even want to bother with me?" I retorted, hoping that logic would free me from an inevitably painful confrontation.

Such hopes were vanquished in an instant as Crawford gripped my shirt with both hands and slammed me up against the locker. "After school, dickhead, at the football stadium!" he snarled. "Be there!"

As he and the others left, I was only sure of one thing. At least I knew where *not* to be after school.

Besides, today was the first day of my six-month grounding. I couldn't be late for that.

Halfway through fourth period English, I was summoned from class by a teacher's aide who informed me that Mr. Brisky, the Dean of Boys, wanted to see me. About what, I wondered, as I followed her down the hall. Perhaps it was the skirmish in the hallway. Somebody must have reported it. More punishment, I thought. It didn't matter in this setting whether you were the victim or the perpetrator, everyone was punished equally. I could just see myself having to serve detention, along with being grounded.

Mr. Brisky was a medium-sized, slender, dark-haired man with hair combed straight back. Although he was only in his mid-to-late thirties, he had a substantial paunch. He spoke in a high falsetto, but that did not negate the authority with which he told me to take a seat. Sitting down, I looked around his office and saw that I was the only one there besides Mr. Brisky. John, Bill, and Kevin were conspicuously absent. Did this mean the victim was the only culprit? Probably. Over the years I had gotten use to absurdities such as these. However, I was totally unaware of the bombshell that was to follow.

Mr. Brisky looked at me intently. "Daryl," he said. "I'm going to cut right to the chase. Did you get a girl pregnant?"

His words sent shock waves coursing through my body.

"Did I *what?*" I asked in amazement.

"Denial is only going to make matters worse," he warned me. "The best thing you can do at this point is own up to your mistake like a man. Tell the truth. Did you get a girl pregnant?"

"No," I replied indignantly.

"Daryl," he said, not bothering to hide his disgust, "I was hoping you'd be man enough to own up to your guilt, but I see you're as big a wimp as everyone says you are."

"When you asked me the question, I assumed that I had a choice of answering yes or no." I replied flatly. "But it appears I'm already assumed guilty. I did not get anyone pregnant! And I resent the accusation!"

"Daryl, we have a girl in the next room with the Dean of Girls," he told me. "She's identified you as the child's father. This is one mistake you cannot run away from."

"Who is she?"

"Feigning ignorance is not going to save you, either."

"But I really don't know who she is!"

"I'm sure the name Charlene Compton rings a bell?!

"Never heard of her."

"Mr. MacGregor, this is the mother of your child. Don't you have any sense of responsibility?"

"Not in this case," I assured him. "I don't know any Charlene Compton, and I did not get any girl pregnant. I don't even go out with girls!"

"All right. I see we're going to have to do this the hard way. Mr. MacGregor, if you will step this way"

I followed him to the Dean of Girls' cubicle where Mrs. Frampton and a blond who was vaguely familiar were waiting.

"Mrs. Frampton," Mr. Brisky said, "here is the father."

"Is this the boy?" Mrs. Frampton asked the girl.

"Yes," she said, glancing first at me and then at Mrs. Frampton, as though waiting for a cue.

"Well, Mr. MacGregor," said Mr. Brisky turning back to me, "what do you say now?"

"The same thing I said before: don't know her, didn't do it. May I go now?"

I thought I'd never get out of that office. She wasn't a bad-looking girl—blond hair, about five feet six inches tall, well-proportioned. If she was pregnant it didn't show, at least, not yet. She appeared to be a bit on the timid side, perhaps even scared. I could empathize with that. But I wasn't about to take on another person's problems. My principle concern was coping with my own. Mr. Brisky had informed me that I had not heard the last of this issue and sternly rebuked me for my "craven lack of principles" and refusal to own up to my responsibilities. I, in turn, had tried to tell him that they weren't mine to own up to, but he just stared at me in quiet disbelief.

When the school day finally came to an end, it was time for me to head straight home and begin serving my six-month grounding, thankful that the football stadium was in the opposite direction. I always tried to be an obedient son – especially when matters pertaining to my health were at risk — I scurried across the bridge that extended over the autobahn and hurried along the path that led me homeward. In an attempt to expedite my journey, I cut through the wooded area just along the outskirts of the apartment complexes, which, as it turned out, was a big mistake. Waiting for me in the clearing were John, Bill, and Kevin.

In an attempt to take evasive action, I tripped over a protruding rock. In seconds, they were upon me. Kevin grabbed me by my jacket and pinned my arms behind me. Crawford's fists slammed against my face, tearing at my flesh, releasing a warm flow of blood that poured into my eyes, out my noise and mouth, and down my face. He leveled a few massive blows to my abdomen, expelling the oxygen I desperately needed in order to endure this ordeal. It was then that Kevin released my arms and threw me to the ground face down and the three of them began to kick me. It seemed a very long time before I heard Bill say, "Okay, he's had enough. Let's go."

As soon as I was sure they had gone, I tried to get up but my legs wouldn't support me, and I fell to the ground spitting blood. I must have passed out, because the next thing I knew, it was dark. Gathering up my books, I realized that I was too dizzy to walk. Falling to my knees, I proceeded to crawl very slowly up the hill that led to my home. Once at the top, I managed to stagger to my feet and cross the road. It occurred to me that all I needed now was for a streetcar to hit me. Of course if I had any inkling of what was to follow, a streetcar might have been viewed as a providential act of mercy.

I was just closing the door behind me when my mother called, "Who's there?"

Before I could answer, she appeared, hair disheveled, her housecoat clutched around her. "What in the name of heaven …"

"Three of the big boys got to me, …" I began and then found that I could say no more. I had neither the will nor the energy to recount what had happened to me, nor did I possess the vigor needed to expel the lactic fluid crying would entail.

"Who were they?" she demanded. "We have to

report this!"

"No!" I said with a voice that was trembling. "It would just make it worse!"

"Well, look at you! We've got to do something! We've got to get you to the infirmary!" She broke off as a key rattled in the lock.

The door opened, and standing there in full uniform were my father and a slightly older soldier sporting silver eagle insignias on his shoulders. It was he who grabbed me by my shirt and started shouting, "What did you do to my daughter, you little bastard?!"

My father placed his hand firmly on the colonel's shoulder and said, "Sir, with all due respect, this is my son, and if you don't take your hands off of him this instant, so help me, I'll deck you hard!"

It was at this point that I experienced a moment of elation. My father was actually standing up for me.

The colonel turned and faced my father. "Are you threatening your commanding officer, MacGregor?" he spat out the words.

"Where my son's concerned, you're damn right I am! Nobody backs my son up against the wall and calls him a bastard! No one except me."

He pushed me against the wall. "All right, you little bastard! I've about had my fill of you!" he shouted. "First you disrespect the fuckin' flag and get me in trouble with my CO, and then you go and knock up my CO's daughter! I ought to kick your ass clean up to your shoulder blades!"

Disappointment overwhelmed me, and tears came to my eyes.

"But I didn't do it!" I cried.

"I'm already mad as hell, boy!" he shouted. "Don't make things any worse by lying!"

"But I'm telling you the truth!"

"Oh, no! This is one thing you can't run away from! So at least own up to it!"

Just then my mother came between us. "Hold it, you two!" she cried. "Look at his face! Are you so angry that you can't see what is right in front of your eyes?"

"What are you talking about?" Father demanded, looking back distractedly.

"You always were one to overlook the obvious! Take a look at Daryl's face! Look at his clothes! He needs medical attention! I'm taking him to the infirmary!"

She began to put on her coat.

A look of dawning concern then came over my father's face. He stepped back and looked me up and down. "I'll drive," he said. He then turned toward Colonel Compton. "Colonel, as you can see, we have a slight emergency on our hands, something we need to tend to right away. But we will be in the general's office tomorrow at fifteen-thirty hours."

"The general?" my mother exclaimed.

"Yes," replied Colonel Compton. "It appears that a matter of this proportion demands the general's service as an intercessor."

"Oh, my God!" cried my mother, turning to me. "What have you gotten us into?"

"I didn't do anything!" I cried. "Why doesn't anybody believe me?"

"Oh, hush!" my mother scolded me in a low voice. "Don't make things any worse by lying! First things first. We're taking you to the infirmary."

I really didn't care at this point. Shock must have been setting in.

Despite the extent of my injuries, the next day found me attending classes. After all, as my father put it, "If you're old enough to take part in adult pleasures, you're old enough to withstand adult pain." Before leaving that morning for school, I received stern instructions to meet both my parents as soon as school let out. It was at that time that we were all to face the general.

Aside from the many off-the-wall comments I received regarding my bruised appearance, the day went by like any other school day. Michele Tenzer was again in top form. "What's the matter, Daryl?" she said in her usual goading way. "You and your lady friend have a lover's quarrel?"

"Knock it off," I retorted. "I'm in no mood for this today!"

"Ohhh!" she mocked me. "Little boy's sounding rough! I warned you what too much sex would do."

The other kids in the class tittered.

"Mercy," I said in a pleading tone. "I'm begging you for mercy."

"Ahh!" She waved her hand dismissively.

The rest of the day proceeded rather uneventfully. I attended all my classes with the exception of P.E. Excusing myself from that class; I headed for the nurse's office. The nurse turned out to be the only amiable personality I had seen in the past two days. However, a voice inside of me warned me not to tell her too much. After all, given the way things had been going for me lately, I was in no position to trust even a friend.

When three o'clock finally arrived, I collected my books, placed them in my satchel, and started home. Before I could reach the bridge that crossed the autobahn, I felt a hand push me from behind. I fell to the ground, landing on my satchel, and looked up to see that John, Kevin, and Bill were standing over me. In anticipation of a fight, a crowd of students began gathering around us.

"Get up, fairy!" John shouted.

"There's three of you and one of me," I said defiantly. "Last night, between the three of you I got a messed up face, a cracked rib cage, four contusions, and eighteen bruises. Do you think you can handle me now?"

To my surprise, everyone but my persecutors began to laugh.

"Shit," said John signaling to Kevin and Bill. "Let's go, guys. This guy ain't even worth beating up."

The crowd began to disperse, except for one guy who yelled, "Fight! Fight! I wanna see a fight!"

Hearing this, John Crawford leaped after the guy, kicking him in the rear end, hitting him in the face, and yelling angrily, "You wanna see a fight? Okay, motherfucker! You're gonna see it firsthand!"

The crowd began to gather again. As for me, I walked the other way. As I distanced myself from the altercation, I could see faculty members arriving. However, as I discovered later, Crawford and friends would be dealt with leniently. In the fortress, confrontations such as these were considered quite commonplace, and discipline that was too stringent was deemed detrimental to a young man's spirit.

The general's office was an elaborately built structure with a lush interior comprised of plush carpeting, regal furnishing and décor, all befitting someone of such high rank and status. The occupant of this stately office building was one Brigadier General Thomas Fenton Cooper, a West Point graduate whose illustrious career dated back prior to the beginnings of World War II. Now, as he approached his thirtieth year of military service, he had hoped to acquire a seat in the Pentagon. But no such luck. For some reason, his "friends" had deserted him and handed him instead, the task of commanding this obscure overseas military base. Here he had to resign himself to such dubious tasks as the one presently before him—presiding over the family matters of base personnel. It was not a task he relished; yet one he would assume with the officious decorum his office prescribed.

When we entered General Cooper's office, I could see Colonel Compton, his wife, and his daughter already seated to the right of the general's desk.

"I swear, Charlene!" her father said, glancing over distainfully at me, "sometimes, I don't think I even know you! All the effort your mother and I put in to your upbringing! It's bad enough you had to go and get yourself in this kind of mess! But of all the boys you had to do it with, why'd you have to pick such a loser!"

I cringed.

"Now, dear," Mrs. Compton said, "you were the one who told her to quit flirting with the enlisted men."

"I know, but …"

"I realize my son may not be any prize at this point," my father broke in, "but you'd better table such remarks or…"

"Gentlemen, gentlemen," General Cooper interrupted them. "This is a general's office, not a boxing ring. Now, we can address the issue here, or we can go to the gym and the two of you can duke it out there. Just be sure you're out of uniform when you do. Otherwise, you'll be committing a court martial offense. Now, I've gone over your records and have familiarized myself as much as possible with the matter at hand."

Then he turned to me.

"Young man," he said, "I hope you realize how serious this matter is that you are facing."

"I didn't do anything!"

I didn't know what else I could say. I felt completely overwhelmed.

"Daryl," my father said, "it's time you faced this like a man!"

"Listen to your father, son," General Cooper told me officiously. "This is not a matter you can just walk away from, not when, because of you, a new life is about to come into this world."

As General Cooper continued pontificating, I heard the slamming of doors and the clatter of footsteps outside. Suddenly, the door flung open and a tall, blond GI uniformed in fatigues with a Spec Four insignia on his sleeve, stormed in, closely followed by the general's administrative aide.

"General!" the flustered aide gasped, "I tried to stop him but …"

The GI boldly approached Colonel Compton, rendering a hasty salute, and in an emphatic tone said "Colonel! I don't care what you do to me! I love your daughter and I want to marry her! I'm the father of her child and I hope you can respect that … Sir!"

Recognition that Charlene had used me to protect her GI boyfriend dawned on everyone. Silence reigned. And then the Colonel spoke.

"Well," the Colonel spoke gruffly, "you're certainly a better picture of what we raised our daughter to look for in a man." And then, turning to General Cooper, "Request permission to be dismissed, sir. We have some family matters to discuss."

General Cooper heaved a sigh of relief. "Certainly, Virgil," he said as they exchanged hasty salutes.

"Well, young man," General Cooper said to me after the Comptons and the GI had left the office, "I hope you've learned something from all this!"

"I'm sure he has," my father answered for me.

I found these admonishing utterances to be absurdly hilarious. In my naiveté, I had actually expected General Cooper to say, "I'm sorry." But, silly me, I could see his proffering of an apology to me would definitely be an appalling affront to his dignity.

However, I had no intention of letting my father get off scott-free. "I believe an apology is in order, Dad," I said as we headed for the car.

My father turned and glared at me with a look that could have frozen snow. "I've had just about enough out of you!" he shouted. "Get in the car!"

I felt like I had been kicked in the stomach. "No, thank you!" I retorted defiantly. "I'll walk."

I turned and ran down the hill, oblivious to the pain that was hammering away at my rib cage.

"Daryl!" Father yelled at the top of his lungs. "You get back here this instant or so help me I'll ..."

I turned and made a hurried backward glance. It was then I saw my mother, always consistent in her role as the intercessor, placing her hand gently upon my father's shoulder as if to say, "Dear, let him go. Now is not the time for punishment."

I continued to run. Rage enveloped every fiber of my being — rage that was all encompassing, all consuming — rage that demanded expression, yet was curtailed by the constraints imposed on me by my rigid upbringing — constraints that made my desire for justice or revenge impatient. Once in the woods, I screamed until my throat was raw. It was nearly ten, long past retreat, when the penetrating chill of the night, coupled with the pains and discomforts brought about by my injuries, conspired to convince me to surrender. Creeping, undetected, into the house, I fell into bed wrapped in a shroud of exhaustion. The next morning at breakfast, my father would not speak to me directly. Anything he had to say to me, he did so through my mother.

The day at school passed rather uneventfully. The few people I had contact with spoke to me as if nothing had happened, and Michele continued to exude a casual derision that she did not even try to contain. As for Crawford and company, they ignored me, which was okay by me. I never did receive an apology from Mr. Brisky. Like all the others in elevated positions of authority, he no doubt felt that any admission of having been wrong would be interpreted as a sign of weakness.

I, however, still seethed with anger at the injustice of it all. It was becoming increasingly clear to me that society in general did not deserve either my trust or respect.

About a week after the ordeal in the general's office, my father received word that he was being deployed to Vietnam in six weeks. He explained that that was all the time we had to get everything in order. I would need to accelerate my studies so I could complete the tenth grade in the time allotted. Mother would need to take care of the sorting and packing, while Father would attend to travel arrangements and other details that were integral to being part of a military bureaucracy. He concluded by saying, "Daryl, I've seen you moping and grousing over what's happened this past week. As of right now, all of that comes to an end! It's over! I don't want to hear any more about it! As far as we're concerned, it never happened! We're heading back stateside."

So that was it. Everything I had gone through had never happened.

I was able to accelerate a major portion of my studies, with the exception of biology. Meanwhile, our home was again in a state of chaos as we tried to pull things together for our move. Once we finally arrived at our destination I was promptly enrolled in summer school so I could work off the incomplete I'd received in biology.

When the time came for Father to depart for Vietnam, military protocol once again carefully orchestrated our farewells. I didn't want to go to the airport, but mother insisted. "Your father is going off on a dangerous assignment," she told me, "and there's always the chance that this might be the last time you see him!"

I smiled inwardly at the thought.

Of course, we did see him again in an even more impressive manifestation since, while in Vietnam, he was awarded a bronze star, a purple heart, and a distinguished service medal, as proof of which we had been sent a photograph of General William Westmoreland presenting him with these awards and shaking his hand. I also caught wind of rumors regarding extramarital dalliances with Southeast Asian women and was later to learn that these flings comprised only a few of many such occurrences, some of which resulted in illegitimate offspring that he had left scattered about the globe. At that distant moment in my life, it became clearer to me why he did not believe for one minute any of my pleas of innocence regarding his CO's daughter.

About three years later, as I was embarking upon my first year of college, I saw, in one of my father's army journals, an item indicating that a John Crawford had received a silver star and a purple heart which was, I thought, ironic, although just the sort of thing to be expected by the military. As for me, I was drafted into the service in the middle of my second year of college, but was expelled on a section-eight psychiatric discharge during basic training, due no doubt in good part to the fact that during my brief stint with Uncle Sam, I found every person in authority to be clones of my father.

Thinking back, I can see that, thanks to the rigidity of the military and my father's refusal to remember anything he did not want to remember, certain items worked to reinforce my sense of being a nonentity. But the telling of what happened, the setting of the words down on paper, acts, I find, as a catharsis. I no longer hear Taps being played endlessly. And I am determined never again to stand at attention.

But most of all, I intend to remember, and in remembering confirm my own reality.

It all really happened.

THE WAR
COMES HOME

The base wives' club was holding a special meeting in the compound's auditorium that Tuesday afternoon. The nature of the topic at hand guaranteed a large crowd. The prolonged United Nations-sanctioned police action was reaching closure, which meant that a massive number of U.S. troops would be returning home to family and friends. Many troops had endured separations of months; some tours encompassed years. During these intervals of separation, it was speculated that the troops had endured trials and hardships that left profound bodily and psychic scars. As a result, many of the returning soldiers were certain to face adjustment problems. This meeting was to address these issues and to reacquaint the GI's with life stateside.

Although she was not among the wives who resided on the base proper, Laura Porter had decided to attend. She really didn't have time for a meeting of this nature, but something told her that she had better attend, since her husband would be one of the many soldiers returning stateside within a week, after nearly three years of separation.

Given this all-too-familiar set of circumstances,

Laura had taken some personal time off from her job to attend this gathering. It was not the first time she'd had to go to such a meeting and it would not likely be her last. Still, it was never an easy matter to address, and the lingering results of these prolonged separations continued to grate unmercifully on the delicate fabric that comprised a purported love relationship, forever testing her patience and endurance, while extending the boundaries of her creative capacity.

Laura still kept an outwardly youthful veneer by maintaining her original raven black hair and her slender body with the help of dye in the former case and exercise in the latter. Twenty years ago, her mother had warned her of what she could expect if she married a soldier, but youth rarely listens to the counsel of age, and in Laura's case, her mother's warnings fell on deaf ears. Love was in the air, and youthful hormones were surging out of control.

Laura's husband, Lieutenant Colonel Lincoln "Buzz" Porter, was endowed with several traits that might be ascribed to an ideal husband. When not on a tour of duty, he performed his husbandly duties diligently, maintaining the house in a state of excellent repair. Being the consummate handyman, he took great joy not only in fixing things, but working on the car, keeping the yard mowed, and even doing a bit of amateur landscaping. Buzz was also an accomplished athlete who made a point of running several miles a day and working out with weights. To top it off, he was also strikingly handsome, endowed with the body of an Arnold Schwarzenegger and the speed and grace of a Bruce Jenner.

Buzz was also a dedicated father. Seeing their son Rick as the true extension of himself, before Buzz had left for his tour, Rick had successfully passed the tryouts for Little League and Pop Warner football, and further delighted his father by coming home from school with the occasional shiner. "That boy's a regular chip off the old block," he often said.

Of course, being a model father, his pride and devotion equally extended to his other two children. Veronica, his eight-year old daughter, for instance, was the apple of his eye. Before he left for his extended tour of duty, five-year-old Veronica was just beginning ballet lessons, and she looked so darling in her tutu that it was difficult to understand why she had to be dragged to her lessons, kicking and screaming.

Then there was Eileen, their teenage daughter, sweet 16 and never been kissed, or at least, that had been the case when he left. His attitude toward Eileen was, in many ways, reflective of what John Wayne had once told Dean Martin regarding his daughter. "Seeing that she's a girl, she'll never be called upon to serve her country, but I aim to make sure she's proud of all the young men who do." And because she was Buzz Porter's daughter, how could things possibly be any other way?

Laura had the job of keeping the family intact. Holding a degree in business with an emphasis in accounting, she was meticulous in her organization of the family's budget, something that Buzz was either incapable of fathoming, or simply unwilling to do. He would earn the money and it would go into the bank. To his mind, that was as far as his responsibility in financial matters extended. "The money I earn goes to the bank," he always said. "After that, I don't know what happens to it." Whenever the family did reach a period of desperate financial straits, which seemed to happen at regular intervals, Buzz always found a way to withdraw, usually by feigning illness, the symptoms of which became quite real, but would clear up miraculously once the crisis had passed.

This limited mode of operating worked for Buzz while he was under the same roof as the rest of the family, but once his assignments necessitated geographic separation, he'd assume a more active role in financial decision-making, usually by sending two-thirds of his paycheck home and keeping a third for himself. In addition, when a perceived personal need would arise, he harbored no qualms about writing a check against their joint account.

This practice often left the family in some dire financial predicaments. However, upon returning home to face the music, his first impulse was always to blame his wife. Consequently, Laura always took it upon herself to sit down with Buzz and go over the financial records, pointing out the canceled checks with his signature on them. The last time she had done this, Buzz had flown into a fit of rage, yelling, "Goddammit! It wouldn't matter if we were five thousand dollars in the black, it still wouldn't be enough to satisfy you!"

Then, predictable as the sun setting in the west, he went off to the bedroom, claiming that he felt sick, leaving Laura to head for an exercise class to work off her frustration.

Laura knew her words fell on deaf ears and that these instances would continue for as long as she stayed married to Buzz. Aware as she was of his extramarital activity when he was gone, she had long ago concluded that such was the nature of the beast. When the little woman was not present to service their need, men took their creature comforts where they could find them, and Buzz was no exception. As the anti-war protestors were carrying signs and placards advocating making love, not war, Laura was consistently contending with the reality that her darling husband, during his separations from home and family, was doing both.

Although there was little that she could do to stop his romantic excursions at the beginning of this past tour, Laura chose to take steps to assure that Buzz's irresponsible spending would not send them into another series of financial setbacks. Cashing in on her business degree, she accepted an accounting assistant position at one of the local firms and set up a separate bank account with only her name on it.

It had now been close to three years since she had joined the firm, and she was presently grossing a higher salary than her officer husband. For once, she knew that Buzz would be returning home to find the finances in good order. Of course, she was not above telling him the reason why that was the case, although that would be a matter for discussion at another time.

Today, the auditorium was packed with the friends and relations of returning servicemen and women. Five speakers occupied seats on the stage; one of these being the president of the base wives' club who served as the hostess. She was a matronly figure, somewhere into her late fifties or early sixties, slightly overweight with gray hair tucked up neatly into a bun. Another speaker was from the staff of the adjutant general's office—a colonel as was Laura's husband, only a bit older and with a receding hairline.

The event also boasted the presence of a popular conservative talk-show host, a short, stocky, talkative man of middle age who was the first to be given the floor. He delivered the same trite platitudes and banalities Laura had heard so many times before.

"Ladies and gentlemen," he began, "I know this is a time for mixed feelings. We're all overjoyed at the prospect of our returning loved ones. Yet, there is a note of sadness we all sense in knowing that the person deboarding that plane in the next few days might not be the same person we saw going off to war. These folks are special. They've all gone off to fight this war to preserve a sacred trust, to keep America safe for democracy, and to assure that it remains the principle bastion of freedom and liberty. What we owe them cannot easily be put into words. But one of the things we do owe them is our love and support. The horrors and hardships they have been made to endure will have most definitely exacted their toll, physically and psychologically, and their adjustment to life stateside will not be an easy one to make."

"To all you wives of servicemen, I have this to say, and I mean it with all sincerity. Many changes might have taken place during the time your husbands have been absent from the family. As the appointed keepers of the home fires, it is your solemn duty to see that these changes are kept to a minimum. Let them know that there is still a sense of sameness... of consistency, something they can still grab hold of. Brief the kids accordingly. All of you should do as much as you can to make him feel that he is returning to the same home he left."

Oh shit! Laura thought, exasperated at the unrealistic expectations she felt placed upon her. How was she supposed to do that? As the speakers droned on, she mentally listed the changes that had taken place during the period of Buzz's absence, and the reactions she would most likely have to face upon his return. The first item was a letter she had received from Buzz a couple of months ago stating that he had torn a cartilage in his right knee while making his daily run of the camp's obstacle course, an indirect result of a grenade explosion that occurred approximately two hundred yards from the course itself, an explosion that turned out to be the beginning of a minor skirmish that was over about as quickly as it began.

Still, because Buzz's injury was incurred in the line of duty, the Army had seen fit to award him a purple heart. Complications from his injury had made both medical and chiropractic treatment necessary, and his ability to run had been impaired. It was, she knew, better than the case of gonorrhea he brought home after one of his other tours of duty, but it was still something he would probably demand that she help him compensate for.

After twenty years of marriage, Laura knew Buzz's idiosyncrasies inside and out, and in the midst of change, she had found Buzz to be very predictable. Whining and complaining, he would expect Laura to cater to his every demand, and the more she gave, the more he would expect.

Next, of course, there were his kids. His "darling little ballerina," Veronica, had hated ballet right from the get-go and had fought Laura every step of the way when it came to donning the tutu and attending dance class until finally, out of frustration, Laura had said, "All right, Veronica! You win. No more ballet! So, what is it you want to do?"

"Sports!" she replied beaming. "I wanna play sports!"

It had not been long afterwards that Veronica's only apparent interest in life was the honing of her athletic skills, with the result that she was successful in making Little League tryouts and soon became the terror of Powder Puff football. She was also quite the scrapper and often came home with more than her fair share of bruises and black eyes. And her language! Laura could not believe the words she heard her little darling using. As for punishment, washing her mouth out with soap only induced an apparent appetite for the stuff.

Laura could just hear what Buzz would say when he became aware of his darling daughter's metamorphosis.

"What have you done with our little girl?" he would say. "She acts like a boy! She doesn't even look like a girl anymore with that short hair! That's not the kind of activity a little girl should be involved with! And what's with the profanity?"

And what about Rick, Buzz's All-American chip off the old block? He was the one who was now wearing the tights and leaping around with the grace of a gazelle. "What the fuck you tryin' to do? Turn my son into some kind of fairy?" was all too likely to be his response. "And I suppose he likes the fellas, too?"

And what about Eileen? Sweet sixteen and never been kissed was now nineteen, attending college in Berkley, living in sin with her twenty-seven year old boy friend, and protesting the war her father had been diligently fighting.

And what was Laura to say in response? She knew Buzz well enough to be certain that he could debate her into the ground. Laura also knew that it was quite unlikely their discussions would be as rational and as succinct as the scenarios she envisioned. In truth, she knew Buzz's responses to the changes that had occurred during his absence would be wildly accusatory and highly irrational. "Can't you do anything right?" he would say. "I leave to go do my patriotic duty for God and country, and I come back and the whole damn family's gone to hell!"

But no matter how often she tried to anticipate what he would say, she was unable to think of anything she could do to stop the uproar that was certain to ensue when he returned to find his hopes for his children shattered. Although she had taken great pains to delicately communicate by both letter and cassette tape these shifts of normalcy as they transpired, Laura knew, by way of Buzz's lack of acknowledgement regarding her communiqué, that he really hadn't heard the messages she was attempting to convey. It was the usual scenario; don't hear, don't acknowledge. Apart from the usual fatherly and romantic platitudes rendered by way of letter and cassette recording during the time of his tour, home was reduced to a distant fantasy.

When the speaker showed signs of droning on forever, Laura got up to leave; it was nothing, after all, she hadn't heard before. Now, more than ever, she wanted to return to her place of gainful employment. At least there she'd felt she could exercise some control over her life.

As the days progressed, she tried riding herd on the kids, telling them to clean up their rooms. She also made attempts to try to restore a semblance of order to the rest of the house. When both these efforts proved futile, she enlisted the aid of domestic help. Perhaps the stress of Buzz's homecoming could be somewhat alleviated if the house was set in proper order. Buzz had always been a stickler for order. She could at least give him that.

When the day of Buzz's homecoming finally arrived, Eileen remained away at college, while Veronica and Rick were tied up with sports and ballet rehearsal, so it was Laura's fate to meet Buzz at the airport alone. Cooling her heels at Arrivals, she waited for still another late flight, something the Army seemed to specialize in.

Given the extended waiting periods, Laura had time to review all the banalities and clichés the briefings had produced. As always, there was a war to fight. With the presence of war, the banner of heroism was given to those who wore the uniforms, while those at home were caught up in the fervor of slogans and catchwords, like "freedom" and "liberty," even though the intent of the overseas skirmishes might have nothing to do with such ideals. And those relegated to the home front were conditioned, like mindless sheep, by the mass media to cheer on the government's efforts, support the troops, keep the home fires burning, and pray for the troops' safe return. All this, knowing full well that, living or dead, the bodies and souls sent over there would not necessarily be the bodies and souls that returned.

Laura reached into her purse and pulled out a worn card that her mother had given her just after her father's funeral. Her mother, too, was in a marriage caught up in a vicious cycle of dysfunction. Laura's father had been an alcoholic; although he had tried to beat his demons, they had ultimately claimed him in the end.

Reflecting on the trials her family had faced as a result of her father's affliction, she began to draw parallels between what was then and what is now. *Was war responsible?* she asked herself. Did it somehow sicken those who took part in it, deaden their minds and usurp their souls? And did the Armed Forces try its best to make family members left behind become enablers?

As the intercom cracked, and the voice announced the arrival of Buzz's plane, Laura read the words aloud, "God grant me the serenity to accept the things I cannot change, the courage to change the things I can, and the wisdom to know the difference."

Summoning up what she could of the elusive commodity known as serenity, and perhaps an even more evasive item known as courage, Laura rose and resolutely headed toward the gate. Peace had been declared. The war had come home.

A LITTER BIT OF WISDOM

Amos Posey, with cane in hand, limped toward the Baskin Robbins ice cream parlor. At the age of eighty, it was his one remaining guilty pleasure, the only item of sustenance his now depleted taste buds could respond to. Upon entering, he ordered a two-scoop dish of his favorite flavor, grabbed a spoon and a handful of napkins, proceeded out the door, and assumed a seat on the patio where a number of other customers were enjoying their own indulgences.

As Amos sat back in his chair, dish in hand, enjoying his ice cream, a gust of wind happened by his seat, scooping up one of the napkins and blowing it to the ground.

A young collegiate upstart with "Green Peace" scrawled across the front of his shirt stepped up to Amos and snapped, "Hey, old man, aren't you gonna pick up that napkin?"

"Nah," Amos replied. "I don't think my old bones and joints could take the strain."

"Man!" the young man replied incredulously. "This is our ecology you're messing with! And you're putting your bones and joints ahead of our environment?"

Amos leaned back in his chair, pushed his spectacles up against his face, and lifted up his knee, cupping it between his folded hands. He said, "Now, see here, young fella! The way I see it, all things happen for a purpose. If the good Lord hadn't o' meant for that napkin to fall on the ground, He wouldn't o' caused that gust of wind to come by. An' ya know something? I don't think the good Lord is through with that napkin. No, sir, I think the good Lord has further plans for that napkin. You might say I think that there napkin is a part of an even greater divine scheme, and my stooping down to pick it up would only gum up the works."

Just as his youthful counterpart was about to address Amos's perceived dubious assumption, another, more powerful burst of wind happened by, blowing the napkin toward the street. As it reached the street, the napkin got caught in an updraft, rose and did multiple aerial summersaults.

"Look over there!" Amos said, pointing at the napkin. "See the wind twirling it about? If that ain't a sign of greater things to come, I don't know what is! And the good Lord's giving us a first hand view of it, even as we're sitting here watching!"

It was shortly after Amos's utterance of those near prophetic words, that another more powerful rush of wind came along, blowing the napkin out of sight of its onlookers. "There she goes." Amos said.

"She's off to fulfill the good Lord's divine purpose and we can only guess at what that purpose might be."

Meantime, a few miles down the road, a brash, husky, tattooed motorcyclist by the name of "Snake" McCutchen, sped down the thoroughfare with the wind blowing fiercely against his face. As Snake raced along, enjoying his perpetual dash of freedom, Amos Posey's runaway napkin happened by, landing on his face, covering his eyes. The split-second occurrence diverted Snake's attention, causing him to swerve over into the opposing lane of traffic where he was struck and killed instantly by an oncoming tractor-trailer rig.

Thus, Amos's speculation had been fulfilled. The napkin did carry out a higher purpose. The good Lord had used a napkin, dropped by an enfeebled consumer of one of life's many delights, to perform a divine function — to call home one of life's wayward travelers to his eternal reward.